"*Come on, Rosy, don't start playing games.*"

The verbal warning was accompanied by a forbidding hooded look that reminded her of former peccadilloes and his merciless punishment of them. Rosy swallowed nervously. It was too late to back out now.

"Guard, I want you to marry me...."

PENNY JORDAN was constantly in trouble in school because of her inability to stop daydreaming—especially during French lessons. In her teens, she was an avid romance reader, although it didn't occur to her to try writing one herself until she was older. "My first half-dozen attempts ended up ingloriously," she remembers, "but I persevered, and one manuscript was finished." She plucked up the courage to send it to a publisher, convinced her book would be rejected. It wasn't, and the rest is history! Penny is married and lives in Cheshire, England.

Penny Jordan's striking mainstream novel *Power Play* quickly became a *New York Times* bestseller. She followed that success with *Silver*, *The Hidden Years*, *Lingering Shadows*, *For Better For Worse* and *Cruel Legacy*.

"Women everywhere will find pieces of themselves in Jordan's characters."

Publishers Weekly on *For Better For Worse*

Don't miss Penny's latest blockbuster, *Power Games*, available 1996.

Books by Penny Jordan

PENNY JORDAN

Unwanted Wedding

Harlequin Books

TORONTO • NEW YORK • LONDON
AMSTERDAM • PARIS • SYDNEY • HAMBURG
STOCKHOLM • ATHENS • TOKYO • MILAN
MADRID • WARSAW • BUDAPEST • AUCKLAND

ISBN 0-373-11821-X

UNWANTED WEDDING

First North American Publication 1996.

Copyright © 1995 by Penny Jordan.

CHAPTER ONE

'GUARD, will you marry me?'

Rosy paced the floor of her bedroom, a fixed, strained expression on her face, her hands gripped into two small fists at her side and her normally clear, guileless dark blue eyes shadowed as she repeated the same four words over and over again under her breath. Even now she still wasn't sure she was actually going to be able to say them out loud.

'Will you marry me? Will you marry me? Will you marry me? Will you marry me?' There, she *had* said it and, even if the words hadn't sounded quite as firm and assured as she would have liked, at least they had been spoken. She was over the first hurdle, she told herself bravely, and if she could manage that one, then she could surely manage the other.

She swallowed hard and looked at the telephone beside her bed. There was no point in shilly-shallying; she might as well get the whole thing over and done with.

But not up here. Not sitting here on her bed in the privacy of her bedroom while she...

Quickly, she averted her eyes from the pretty girlishness of her flower-sprigged bedcover, virginal white with a scattering of flower posies. She had been fourteen the year she had chosen it; she was almost twenty-two now.

5

Twenty-two, but as naïve and unworldly as a girl still—or so she had been told.

Her throat closed nervously. She didn't need to remind herself exactly who it was who had said those words to her.

Quickly, she opened her bedroom door and hurried downstairs. She would use the phone in the room which had been her father's study and, before that, her grandfather's. To say those words in that room would be appropriate somehow, would lend them weight and dignity.

She picked up the receiver and punched in the numbers jerkily, her body tensing as she heard the ringing tone.

'Guard Jamieson, please,' she told the girl on the other end of the line. 'It's Rosy Wyndham.'

As she waited to be connected to Guard she nibbled nervously at her bottom lip—a childhood habit she had thought she had outgrown.

'Only children do that,' Guard had warned her the year she was eighteen. 'Women...'

He had paused then and looked at her mockingly, causing her to ask him unthinkingly, 'Women do what?'

'Don't you really know?' he had quizzed her mockingly. 'Women, my dear, innocent Rosy, only carry these kind of scars——' he had leaned forward then and slowly run the tip of his finger along her swollen bottom lip, with its two small tooth indentations, pausing to touch them in such a way that the sharp *frisson* of sensation that had run through her had actually become an open physical convulsion of her whole body '—when they've been left there by a lover... A very ardent lover...'

Of course he had laughed at the scorching colour that had stained her skin. Guard was like that. In the old days he would have been a freebooter, a pirate—a man who cared for no one and made his own laws, his own rules, so her grandfather had always claimed. Her grandfather, although he would never admit it, had always had something of a soft spot for Guard, Rosy suspected.

'Rosy, what is it? What's wrong?'

The sound of his voice reverberating roughly in her ear caused her to tighten her grip on the receiver as her body rebelled against the knowledge of how unsettling she still sometimes found him— even though, with maturity, she had learned to ignore the taunting, loaded comments with which he still sometimes liked to torment her.

He wasn't like that with other women; with other women he was all sensual charm and warmth, but then, of course, he didn't see her as a woman, only as——

'Rosy are you still there?'

The irritation in his voice jerked her back to reality.

She took a deep breath. 'Yes, I'm still here, Guard... Guard, there's something I want to ask you. I...'

'I can't talk now, Rosy. I've got an important call waiting. Look, I'll call round tonight and we can discuss whatever it is then.'

'No.' Rosy started to panic. What she had to ask him was something it would be far easier for her to say at a safe distance; she thought of asking him to marry her, of proposing to him face to face—— She gave a small, worried gulp, but Guard

had already replaced the receiver and it was too late
for her to tell him now that she didn't want to see
him.

As she replaced her own receiver she stared sadly
around the room.

Four hundred years of history were encapsulated
in this room, this house. It had stood here since
Elizabeth I had bestowed the land on Piers
Wyndham, a gift, so the official story ran, for
courtly services; a gift, so the unofficial one went,
for something far more personal and intimate.

Piers had called the house he had built Queen's
Meadow, in acknowledgement of Elizabeth's gen-
erosity. It wasn't a very grand house, nor even a
generously large one, but in Rosy's view it was certainly far too extravagantly large for one person or
even one family—especially when she knew from
her work at the shelter how many people were
homeless and in desperate need of a roof over their
heads.

'So what would you do, given free choice?'
Guard had taunted her the last time she had raised
the subject. 'Turn the place over to them? Watch
them tear out the panelling and use it for firewood;
watch them . . .?'

'That's unfair,' she had protested angrily. 'You're
being unfair . . .'

But even Ralph, who was in charge of the shelter,
had commented on more than one occasion that
she wasn't streetwise enough; that she was too soft-
hearted, too idealistic, her expectations and beliefs
in others far too high. She suspected that Ralph
was inclined to despise her, and at first he had certainly been antagonistic towards her, deriding her

background and her accent, condemning her comparative wealth and lifestyle and comparing it to those of the people who used the shelter.

'Makes you feel better, does it,' he had jeered, 'spending your time doing good works?'

'No, it doesn't,' Rosy had told him honestly. 'But my money—my wealth, as you call it—is in trust and I can't touch the capital even if I wanted to. If I found a "proper" job, paid work, I'd be taking that job away from someone who needs to earn their living.'

She and Ralph got on much better these days, although he and Guard loathed one another. Or rather Ralph loathed Guard; Guard wasn't human enough to allow himself to feel that kind of emotion about anyone. In fact, she sometimes doubted that Guard had ever felt a human emotion in his entire life.

She knew how much Ralph resented having to go cap in hand to Guard for money towards running the shelter, but Guard was the wealthiest man in the area, his business the most profitable.

'He's a very rare combination,' her father had once told her. 'An entrepreneur—successfully so— and an honest man as well, highly principled.'

'An arrogant bastard,' was what Ralph called him.

'Sexy,' was what one of Rosy's old school-friends had breathed enthusiastically when she had come down to pay Rosy a visit. Married, and bored with her husband already, apparently, she had eyed Guard with an open, hungry greed that Rosy had found not just embarrassing, but somehow humiliating as well. It was as though Sara, with the hot, burning looks she was constantly throwing Guard's way, the none-too-subtle hints and sexual innuendoes, the physical contact of deliberately contrived touches, was somehow underlining her own sexual immaturity, and reinforcing all the taunts that Guard had ever made about her.

She was well aware that Guard thought her naïve and unawakened—but so what? All right, so his comments and taunts might fluster and sometimes even hurt her, but she had made a vow to herself a long time ago that she was not going to rush into a sexual relationship before she was ready for it; that she was not going to experiment with sex for sex's sake; that when she finally explored the world of her own sexuality it would be with a partner who felt as she did, a man who loved her and who was not ashamed to acknowledge that fact and with whom she could let down her guard and reveal the vulnerable, romantic, loving side of her nature.

So far she had not met that man, but when she did, she would know him, and she was not, after all, in any hurry. She was only twenty-one. Twenty-one and still a virgin. Twenty-one and about to propose marriage to Guard, who was most definitely not anything of the kind and who——

She glanced at her watch. Four o'clock. She knew that Guard often didn't leave his office until well after everyone else had gone, which meant it could be seven o'clock or even eight before he came round. All those hours to wait. All those hours nerving herself to deliver her proposal.

What would he say? Laugh himself silly, no doubt. Her face burned hotly with chagrin at the thought.

It was all her solicitor's fault, she decided crossly. If Peter hadn't suggested——

She walked over to the window, remembering Peter's last words to her before he left: 'Promise me that you'll at least ask him, Rosy.'

'Sacrifice myself to save this place? Why should I?' she had demanded angrily. 'It isn't even as though I *want* the house. You know how I feel . . .'

'You know what will happen if Edward inherits it,' Peter had countered. 'He'll destroy this place simply for the pleasure it will give him.'

'And to get back at Gramps. Yes, I know that,' Rosy had agreed.

Edward was her father's cousin; he and her grandfather had quarrelled long before Rosy was born—a bad quarrel over money and morals which had resulted in her grandfather's banning Edward from ever setting foot inside the house again.

Every family had its black sheep; theirs was no exception. Even now, in middle age, despite his outward air of respectability, his marriage and his two sons at prep school, there was something unpleasant about Edward.

He might never have actually broken the law in his financial dealings, but he had certainly crossed over the line under cover of darkness on one or more occasions, her father had often stated.

Her father.

Rosy turned her attention away from the window and looked towards the desk. Her father's photograph was still on it. The one he had had taken in uniform shortly before his older brother's death.

He had left the army then and come home to be with his father—he had been no stranger to death himself since the death of Rosy's mother.

Queen's Meadow had meant everything to them, her father and her grandfather. She loved the house, of course—who could not do?—but she felt no sense of possessiveness towards it, far from it.

It wasn't pride she felt as she walked through its rooms, but guilt.

If only things had been different. If only Edward had been different, she could have so happily and easily have walked away from here and bought or rented herself a small place in town and given all her time and attention to working at the shelter.

But how could she do that now?

'Edward will destroy this place,' Peter had warned her. 'He'll tear the heart out of it, sell off everything that's worth selling, and then he'll tear it down brick by brick and sell off the land to one of his cronies who'll——'

'No, he can't do that,' she had protested. 'The house is listed and——'

'And, knowing Edward, he won't find it at all difficult to find someone who's willing to claim that they misunderstood the instructions they were given. Just how long do you think this place could stay standing once it was assaulted by half a dozen determined men with bulldozers? And of course Edward would make sure that nothing could be connected with him. He hated your grandfather, Rosy, and he knew how much Queen's Meadow meant to him and to your father.'

'Too much,' Rosy had sighed. 'No, this place is an anachronism, Peter. No matter how beautiful it is, for one family to live in a house this size... Oh, why couldn't Gramps have listened to me and deeded it to a charity? Why couldn't he?'

'So you don't care what happens to the house? You don't mind Edward inheriting it and destroying it, destroying four hundred years of history?'

'Of course I mind,' Rosy told him fretfully. 'But what can I do? You know the terms of that idiotic will Gramps made as well as I do. In the event of both his sons predeceasing him, the house and his estate go to the closest of his blood relatives to be married within three months of his death and capable of producing an heir. He made that will years ago after Uncle Tom died, and if Dad hadn't——'

She had broken off then, her throat choked with tears. Her father's death so unexpectedly from a heart attack just weeks before her grandfather had slid from a coma and into death was something she still hadn't fully come to terms with.

'Edward fulfils all the terms of that will and he——'

'*You* are your grandfather's closest blood relative,' Peter had reminded her quietly.

'Yes, but I'm not married. And not likely to be, at least not within the next three months,' Rosy had told him drily.

'You could be,' Peter had told her slowly, 'with an arranged marriage. A marriage entered into specifically so that you could fulfil the terms of your grandfather's will. A marriage which could be brought to an end very easily and quickly.'

'An arranged marriage?' Rosy had stared blankly at him. It sounded like something out of one of her favourite Georgette Heyer novels; fine as the theme for a piece of romantic froth, but totally implausible in reality.

'No,' she had told him impatiently, shaking her head so hard that her dark curls had bounced against her shoulders. Irritably she had pushed them off her face. Her hair was the bane of her life— thick, so dark it was almost black, and possessing of a life of its own.

A little gypsy, her grandfather had often fondly called her. But whenever she had tried to have her wild mane tamed, it had rebelled, and reverted to its tumbling mass of curls almost as soon as she had closed the hairdresser's door behind her, so that eventually she had given up trying to control it.

'It's out of the question and, besides, it takes two to make a marriage—even an arranged one— and I can't think of anyone who——'

'I can.' Peter had anticipated her quietly.

Was she imagining it, or did his words have a slightly ominous ring to them? She paused, shifting her gaze from the Grinling Gibbons carving on the staircase to her solicitor's face, eyeing him suspiciously.

'Who?' she demanded warily.

'Guard Jamieson,' Peter told her. Rosy sat down abruptly on the stairs.

'Oh, no,' she announced firmly. 'No, no, never.'

'He would be the ideal person,' Peter continued enthusiastically, as though she hadn't spoken. 'After all, he's never made any secret of how much he wants this place.'

'Never,' Rosy agreed drily, remembering how often Guard had bombarded her grandfather with requests—demands, almost—that he sell Queen's Meadow to him. 'If Guard wants the house that badly, he can always try to persuade Edward to sell it to him,' she pointed out.

Peter's eyebrows rose. 'Come on, Rosy. You know that Edward hates Guard almost as much as he did your grandfather.'

Rosy sighed.

'Yes,' she agreed. It was true. Guard and Edward were old business adversaries and, as her father had stated on more than one occasion, there hadn't been a confrontation between the two men yet out of which Guard had not come the winner. 'The mere fact that he knows how much Guard loves this place would only add to his pleasure in destroying it.'

'We're only talking about a business arrangement between the two of you, you know, some simple basic formalities which would enable you to fulfil the terms of the will. In time the marriage could be dissolved. You could sell the house to Guard and——'

'In time? How much time?' she had asked him suspiciously.

'A year—a couple of years...' Peter had shrugged, ignoring her dismayed gasp. 'After all, it isn't as though you want to marry someone else, is it? If you did, there wouldn't be any problem, any need to involve Guard.'

'I can't do it,' she told Peter positively. 'The whole idea is completely ridiculous, repulsive.'

'Well, then, I'm afraid you'll have to resign yourself to the fact that Edward will inherit. Your grandfather's already been dead for almost a month.'

'I can't do it,' Rosy repeated, ignoring Peter's comment. 'I could never ask *any* man to marry me, but especially not Guard...'

Peter had laughed at her.

'It's a business proposal, that's all. Think about it, Rosy. I know how ambivalent your feelings towards Queen's Meadow are, but I can't believe that you actually want to see Edward destroy it.'

'No, of course I don't,' Rosy had agreed.

'Then what have you got to lose?'

'My freedom?' she had suggested hollowly.

Peter had laughed again. 'Oh, I doubt that Guard would interfere with that,' he had assured her. 'He's much too busy to have time to worry about what you'll be doing. Promise me that you'll at least think about it, Rosy. It's for your sake that I'm doing this,' he had added. 'If you let Edward destroy this place, you're bound to feel guilty.'

'The way you do for putting all this moral blackmail on me?' Rosy had asked him drily.

He had had the grace to look slightly uncomfortable.

'All right, I'll think about it,' she had agreed.

And ultimately she had done more than just think about it, Rosy acknowledged, as she dragged her thoughts back to the present.

'The trouble with you is that you're far too soft-hearted.' How often had she heard that accusation over the years?

Too often.

But Peter was right. She couldn't let Edward destroy Queen's Meadow without at least making some attempt to save it. By sacrificing herself. A wicked smile curled her mouth, her eyes suddenly dancing with bright humour. Oh, how chagrined Guard would be if he could read her mind. How many women were there who would look upon marriage to him in that light? Not many. Not *any*, she admitted, at least not from what she heard.

Well, all right, so she was peculiar—an oddity who for some reason could not see anything attractive in that magnetic sexuality of his which seemed to obsess virtually every other female who set eyes on him. So she was immune to whatever it was about him that made other women go weak at the knees, their eyes glazing with awe as they started babbling about his sexy looks, his smouldering eyes, his mouth and its full, sensual bottom lip, his shoulders, his body, his awesome charismatic personality, his single state and the subtle aura not just of sexual experience, but of sexual expertise which clung to him like perfume to a woman's body.

Oddly, the last thing that most of them mentioned about him was his wealth.

Well, she could see nothing remotely sexually attractive about him, Rosy decided crossly, and she never had. As far as she was concerned, he was an arrogant, sarcastic pig who enjoyed nothing more than making fun of her.

Only last month at a dinner party, when the hostess had been remarking to her that the male cousin she had had visiting her had begged her to seat him next to Rosy at dinner, Guard, who had

overheard their hostess's remark, had leaned over
and said sardonically, 'Well, if he's hoping to find
a woman somewhere under that mass of hair and
that very unflattering outfit you're wearing, Rosy,
he's going to be very disappointed, isn't he?'

Since the 'unflattering outfit' he referred to had
been a very carefully chosen collection of several
different layers of softly toning shades of grey, all
determinedly hunted down in a variety of charity
shops, carried home triumphantly and repaired and
laundered, Rosy had shot him an extremely bitter
look.

'Not all men judge a woman on how she per-
forms in bed, Guard,' she had told him through
gritted teeth.

'Luckily for you,' he had responded, not in the
least bit fazed by her retaliation. 'Because, ac-
cording to all the gossip, you wouldn't have the
faintest idea what to do there.'

She had flushed, of course, the hot colour
crawling betrayingly over her skin, not so much because of what he had said—after all, she was not
ashamed of the fact that she was not prepared to
jump into bed with every man who asked her—but
because of the way Guard was watching her, because of the amusement and mockery in his eyes,
because, oh, so shamingly and appallingly, just for
a second, she could actually almost *see* him in bed
with some anonymous woman, his body bare and
brown, his hands stroking the woman's paler, softer
skin while she clung to him with small, pleading
sounds of need...

She had blinked away the vision immediately, of
course, telling herself that it must have had some-

thing to do with the sexy film she and a friend had been discussing earlier in the day.

She and Guard had continued their argument later in the evening, just before Guard had left with the extremely glamorous and elegant-looking blonde who was accompanying him.

'Anyway,' Rosy had told him, her small chin jutting out defiantly as she felt herself losing ground, 'it makes sense these days *not* to have too many sexual partners.'

'The present climate is certainly a convenient hedge to hide behind,' Guard had agreed suavely. 'Especially when...'

'Especially when what?' Rosy had challenged him.

'Especially for you,' he had told her blandly.

The return of his companion had prevented Rosy from saying anything else.

An arranged marriage with Guard. She *must* have been mad to let Peter talk her into such a crazy idea. But he *had* talked her into it and she couldn't back out now. Did Guard want Queen's Meadow enough to agree? Half of her hoped not. And the other half...

'All right, Rosy, what's this all about? And if you're after another donation to that charity of yours, I'm warning you that right now I'm not feeling in the most generous of moods...'

Dumbly Rosy watched Guard walk into the hall. Her heart was beating so heavily it felt as though it was going to force its way through her chest wall.

She couldn't remember ever, ever feeling so nervous before—not even when Gramps had found out about her sneaking out at night to go poaching with Clem Angers. She had had Guard to thank for that, of course, and——

Firmly, she brought her thoughts back to the present.

Guard was slightly earlier than she had expected, and if the sight of him wearing the expensively tailored dark suit with its equally expensive, crisp white cotton shirt had not been one that was already familiar to her, she suspected she would have found it extremely daunting.

But then Guard *could* be daunting, even when he was casually dressed, she acknowledged, and it wasn't just because of his height, nor even because of those broad shoulders and that tautly muscular physique over which her female friends cooed and sighed so stupidly, either.

There was something about Guard himself—an air, a manner, a certain intangible something—that set him slightly apart from other men, made him stand out from other men, an aura of power and control, of...of sheer maleness, so potent that even she was acutely aware of it, she admitted. Aware of it, but not attracted by it, she reminded herself sharply. *She* could never be attracted by Guard; he was not her kind of man. She liked men who were softer, warmer—more approachable, more...more human, less...less sexual?

Nervously, she cleared her throat.

'What's wrong?' Guard asked her drily. 'You're staring at me like a rabbit at a dog.'

'I'm not afraid of you,' Rosy retorted, stung.

'I'm extremely glad to hear it. Look, I'm due to fly out to Brussels in the morning, Rosy, and I've got a briefcase full of documents to read before I do. Just tell me what you want, there's a good girl, and don't start backtracking now and telling me it isn't important. We both know that there's no way you'd get in touch with me if it weren't.'

The irony in his voice made her frown slightly but he was watching her impatiently, unfastening his jacket, reaching up to loosen the knot in his tie.

As she focused on the movement of his hands, she could feel the knot in her stomach tightening.

'Come on, Rosy, don't start playing games. I'm not in the mood for it.'

The verbal warning was accompanied by a forbidding, hooded look that reminded her of former peccadilloes and his merciless punishment of them.

She swallowed nervously. It was too late to back out now.

Screwing up her courage, she took a deep breath.

'Guard, I want you to marry me . . .'

CHAPTER TWO

Rosy had automatically closed her eyes as she spoke, but in the silence that followed her stammered request she was forced to open them again.

'What did you say?'

The words, evenly spaced out and ominously soft, were snapped out between Guard's strong white teeth, and he was looking at her as though it was her bones, her body, he would really like to inflict that punishment on, she recognised nervously as she cleared her throat a second time.

'I—I asked you if you'd marry me,' she repeated quickly, suppressing her body's physical instinct for flight.

'Is this some kind of joke?'

He sounded very angry, Rosy recognised, which rather surprised her. She had spent most of the last few hours trying to envisage exactly what his reaction to her request was going to be. That he might be angry had never even entered her head. Amusement, mockery, contempt, disdain, an outright refusal—all of these things she had expected, but anger . . .

'No, it isn't a joke,' she told him, adding grimly under her breath, 'I only wish it were.

'It was Peter's idea,' she continued doggedly. 'I told him it was crazy, but he says it's the only way we can stop Edward from inheriting the house and destroying it. You know the terms of Gramps' will.'

'I know them,' Guard agreed, 'but I hadn't realised this place meant so much to you that you'd be prepared to fulfil them. What happened to all that insistence that you weren't going to marry until you fell in love, until you were sure that your love was returned? Or was that just a girlish fantasy that faded in the reality of losing this place?'

'No, it wasn't,' Rosy told him angrily, 'but...'

He had taken off his jacket and gone to stand in front of the huge, open fireplace which, along with the Grinling Gibbons carving on the stairs, dominated the hallway.

Guard suited the house, Rosy recognised, before hurriedly looking away from him. With his height and the aura of power and authority which he wore with much the same swagger and flair with which her original ancestor must have worn his cloak, he looked much more at home here than she did herself.

The large rooms, the dark panelling, overshadowed her. In looks and build she took more after her mother's family than her father's. Whereas most of the portraits of her ancestors showed stocky, sturdy-looking individuals, she was small and slender—thin, Guard had once disparagingly called her.

It was still *her* home, though, and a part of her, much as she was reluctant to admit it, would hate to see it destroyed. She was honest enough to recognise that, despite her own feelings towards Guard, the house would be safe in his hands.

'But what...?' he demanded. 'But you love this place so much that you can't bear to give it up? But you love me so much that...?'

He threw the last question mockingly at her, already knowing the answer, but Rosy still gave it to him.

'No, of course not,' she denied vehemently.

Why was he looking at her like that? Watching her with those hooded, eagle-sharp eyes that made her feel so uncomfortable.

'So, you don't love either the house or me, but you're prepared to marry me to keep it.'

'To *save* it,' Rosy corrected him quickly, 'from Edward and... And it would be an arranged marriage,' she added carefully, turning her back slightly towards him. For some reason, she found it easier to talk to him like that. She felt safer knowing that he couldn't see her face, and that she didn't have to see his.

'An arranged marriage. And it needn't last very long. Peter said we could probably even get an annulment and that we need not—— That we wouldn't be——' She broke off awkwardly, so anxiously conscious of the uncomfortable quality of his silence that unwarily she turned round to look at him.

'We wouldn't be what?' he encouraged her mockingly. 'Cohabiting...intimate...having sex... making love...?'

Rosy hated the way he almost caressed the words, rolling them over his tongue, purring over them almost, enjoying every second of her own discomfort, she was sure.

'If that's supposed to encourage me to agree, you don't know very much about the male sex and its ego, Rosy. Do you really think that a man—*any* man—wants to stand up in court and tell the world that he isn't man enough to take his wife to bed? Do you honestly believe that anyone, but most especially that repulsive cousin of yours, is going to believe the fiction that you and I are genuinely husband and wife when the very mention of the word sex is enough to turn you into a physical embodiment of the traditional, trembling, untouched virgin? Oh, no, my dear. If I were crazy enough to agree to this fraudulent marriage of yours—and it's a very big 'if' —in the eyes of the rest of the world it would have to look as though it was very much the real thing, even if that did mean that ultimately, you'd have to undergo the indignity of going through a divorce.'

Rosy's heart had started thumping heavily as he spoke, but when she realised that he wasn't, as she had expected, going to refuse her proposal outright, she stared uncertainly at him, her face still flushed from her earlier embarrassment. It was only Guard who made her react like that when he talked about sex, she admitted crossly. Not even when the teenage boys who used the shelter made what were sometimes extremely blunt and often crude comments did she get as embarrassed or self-conscious as she did with Guard.

'But it wouldn't *be* a real marriage,' she insisted, turning round to focus watchfully on his face. You were supposed to be able to tell what was really in a person's mind from their eyes, but that rule didn't apply to Guard. She could *never* tell what he was thinking. 'I mean, we wouldn't be...'

'Lovers,' he supplied for her. 'It would certainly be very hard to imagine. The only time I've ever held you in my arms, you damned near scratched my eyes out,' Guard reminded her grimly.

'You terrified me,' Rosy defended herself. 'Picking me up like that. It was dark and I...'

'You were out clandestinely with Clem Angers, poaching your grandfather's salmon.'

'Clem had been promising to take me out for ages to show me the badgers' sett. And then *you* had to interfere and spoil everything,' Rosy remembered indignantly. 'He had been promising me that he'd take me just as soon as I was sixteen.'

'Really? I do hope you didn't use that unfortunate turn of phrase when you were explaining what you were doing to your father. Sweet sixteen,' he continued, ignoring the angry flush darkening Rosy's face. 'Sweet sixteen and never been kissed. Just refresh my memory for me, will you, Rosy? *How* old are you now?'

'Twenty-two almost,' she told him impatiently.

'Mmm... and presumably now well-experienced in the art of kissing, if nothing else. You certainly ought to be after the practice session I witnessed last New Year's Eve at the Lewishams' ball.'

Rosy's flush deepened as she remembered the incident he referred to. One of the Lewisham cousins, a rather intoxicated, impressionable young man, who had been gazing adoringly at her from the other side of the dance floor all evening, had caught up with her just as she tried to make her escape, grabbing hold of her in the semi-darkness of the passageway that led to the cloakroom, imprisoning her in his arms for a few brief seconds while he pressed impassioned kisses against her determinedly closed mouth. It had been a harmless enough episode. He had presented himself rather sheepishly and shamefacedly at Queen's Meadow the following afternoon, full of remorse and apologies, and begging for a chance to make a fresh start, which Rosy had tactfully refused. But up until now she had had no idea that Guard had even witnessed the small incident.

She turned away from him, pacing the room edgily.

'Why on earth don't you buy yourself some decent clothes? After all, it's not as though you can't afford it. Your father left you very well provided for. Or wouldn't it impress dear, sanctimonious Ralph if you turned up looking like a woman rather than a half-grown child?'

'Ralph is not sanctimonious,' Rosy denied angrily as she turned to face him. 'And as for my clothes...' She frowned as she glanced down at her well-worn leggings and the thick, bulky sweater which had originally belonged to her father.

'I dress to please myself, in what feels comfortable. Just because *you're* the kind of man who likes to see a woman humiliating herself by dressing up in something so skin-tight she can barely walk in it, never mind run, teetering around in high heels... Mind you, I suppose at your age that *would* be your idea of style,' she added disparagingly.

'I'm thirty-five, Rosy,' Guard reminded her grimly, 'not some ageing fifty-year-old desperately fighting off middle-age, and as for my ideas of style, personally I think there's nothing quite so alluring as a woman who has enough confidence in herself to dress neither to conceal her sexuality nor to reveal it—a woman who wears silk or cashmere, wool or cotton, clothes cut in plain, simple styles—but then *you* aren't a woman yet, are you, Rosy?'

For some reason Rosy couldn't define, his comments, his criticism had hurt her, making her leap immediately to her own defence, her voice husky with emotion as she told him fiercely, 'I *am* a woman, but *you* can't see that. You only think of women in terms of sex—the more sexual experience a woman has had, the more of a woman it makes her. Well, for your information——'

She stopped abruptly. Why was she letting him get to her like this? Why did they always end up quarrelling, arguing, antagonists?

'For my information, what?' Guard challenged her.

'Oh, nothing.' Rosy retreated. She had been a fool to listen to Peter. If, as he said, the only way to save the house was via an arranged marriage, then it would have to be with someone else. *Anyone* else, she decided savagely. Anyone at all just so long as it wasn't the arrogant, hateful, horrid man standing in front of her, watching her with those mesmeric, all-seeing, all-watchful golden eyes.

'All right, I know,' she told him bitterly. 'It was a stupid idea, and I was a fool to think you'd agree, no matter how much you might want Queen's Meadow. I'd be better off advertising in the personal columns for a husband...'

Something flickered briefly in Guard's eyes, a tiny movement so swiftly controlled that Rosy felt she must have imagined it.

'I haven't given you my answer yet.'

Rosy looked up at him.

'You're talking about taking a potentially very dangerous course,' he continued warningly, as Rosy remained silent. 'Edward is bound to be suspicious.'

'But he can't *do* anything. Not so long as I've fulfilled the terms of my grandfather's will.'

'Mmm... Edward is a very tricky character. It wouldn't be wise to underestimate him. There's an element of fraud in this whole plan of yours.'

'Fraud?' Rosy interrupted him anxiously. 'But...'

'I'll be back from Brussels the day after tomorrow. I'll give you my answer then. And, Rosy,' he told her as he turned to leave, 'in the meantime, no ads in the personal columns, hmm?'

It wasn't fair, Rosy reflected indignantly when he had gone. *Why* did he always have to make her feel like a child? And a particularly stupid child at that.

'You've forgotten to put sugar in my coffee again,' Ralph reproved Rosy. He frowned slightly, his sandy eyebrows lifting almost into his hairline as he added, 'In fact you've seemed very preoccupied altogether these last couple of days. Is something wrong?'

'No... no, nothing,' Rosy denied untruthfully.

'Mm. You know, Rosy, it's a pity you didn't work a bit harder at persuading your grandfather to leave Queen's Meadow to us. Hallows, the engineering place, is closing down next month and that's bound to put more pressure on us. God knows how many more it's going to make homeless. We haven't got anything like enough beds here as it is. When I think of that damned big house and all those rooms...'

'Yes, yes I know,' Rosy agreed guiltily. She hadn't discussed with Ralph the terms of her grandfather's will and, since Edward had already made it plain that he expected to inherit the house, Rosy had simply allowed Ralph to believe that as well.

When she had first announced that she was going to do voluntary work at the shelter, she knew her father had been a little concerned but, needless to say, it had been Guard who had taken it upon himself to warn her that, in view of her family connections and her comparative wealth, Ralph might put pressure on her to help fund the shelter.

'Ralph would never do anything like that,' she had protested then, indignantly. And she had believed it . . . *Had* believed it . . . *Still* believed it, and if Ralph was cross with her because he felt she ought to have persuaded her grandfather to leave Queen's Meadow to their charity, well, she could understand why.

She could never walk into the old, run-down shabby building on the outskirts of the town without a small pang.

They all did their best to make it as homely as possible, but the rooms still had that air about them that reminded her of the boarding-school she had attended when she and her father had first returned to England from his army posting in Germany. She hadn't stayed there long, but it had left a lasting impression on her.

The first spring she had worked at the shelter she had arrived one morning with the boot of her small car filled with vases she had 'borrowed' from home and the back seat covered in a mass of daffodils.

Ralph had found her just as she was placing the last vase in position.

She winced even now when she remembered how angry he had been.

'You waste money on flowers when we barely have enough to buy them food,' he had shouted at her.

She had never made the same mistake again, but sometimes the sheer austerity of the shelter weighed her down, her own feelings adding to the compassion and anguish she already felt at the plight of the young people they took in.

Today, though, she was guiltily aware that her mind was more on her own problems than those of the homeless. Guard was due back this afternoon. What would his decision be? What did she *want* his decision to be?

She knew quite well what Ralph would say were she to ask him for his advice, and the modern, aware part of her agreed with him: there were far more important things to worry about than a house; there were people, her fellow human beings, in far more need than a building and yet, when she walked round the house, something she had found herself doing increasingly frequently recently, she was also emotionally aware of the love, the care, the human effort that had gone into making it what it was. It wasn't the material value of the Grinling Gibbons carving on the staircase that smote her with guilt at the thought of its destruction, it was her knowledge of the work, the craftsmanship which had gone into its carving. If she closed her eyes she could almost instantly be there, smell the fresh, pungent odour of the new wood, feel the concentrated silence of the busy apprentices as they watched their master, see the delight and pride in their faces when they were finally allowed to make their contribution, when their work was finally inspected and passed, the experienced hands of the master running critically over their carving while they held their breath and waited for his verdict.

The plasterwork on the ceilings, the furniture in the rooms—all of it had been created with human endeavour, with human pride.

Ralph would no doubt see another side of it, of apprentices injured and maimed, thrown out of work to starve, of workmen paid a pittance by their rich patrons.

'What's up, boyfriend giving you a hard time?'

Rosy turned her head to force a smile in the direction of the thin, pimply boy watching her, ignoring his companion's snigger and clearly audible, 'I'll bet if he was she wouldn't be looking so miserable,' without even a hint of the betraying colour that Guard could conjure so easily with a comment only a tenth as sexual.

'Have you heard anything about that job you went for yet, Alan?' she asked, ignoring both comments.

'Nah... Don't 'spose I'll hear owt, either.'

'You could try getting some qualifications,' Rosy suggested, 'going to night school.'

She already knew what the answer would be and wasn't surprised when the boy shook his head in denial of her comment. When a system had failed you as badly as it had failed these youngsters, it must be hard to have any faith in it, Rosy acknowledged as she watched the two of them swagger off in the direction of the television lounge.

An hour later, as she drove home, her stomach was already cramping at the thought of hearing Guard's decision. To her surprise, as she pulled up at the rear of the house in what had originally been the stable yard, she saw that an unfamiliar car was already parked there.

As she got out of her own car she eyed the bright red Rolls-Royce uncertainly. She went into the house through the back entrance, through a maze of passages, past a cluster of small, dark rooms.

She could hear voices in the front hall and she tensed as she recognised one of them. Edward, her father's cousin. What was he doing here and, more important, how had he got in?

Taking a deep breath, she pushed open the door into the hall.

Edward was standing with his back to her, his bald head shining in the light from the overhead chandelier which he had switched on.

Both he and the man with him were looking up at it.

'Mmm...I suppose it could fetch a tidy bit, although there's not so much call for that sort of thing now. Too big and too expensive. We'd probably be better shipping it abroad, finding an agent——' He broke off as he turned round and saw Rosy, and touched Edward's arm, drawing his attention to her.

'Ah, Rosy...'

Edward's genial manner didn't deceive Rosy. It never had. She shared her grandfather's and her father's dislike and distrust of him.

'What are you doing here, Edward?' Rosy demanded, ignoring his pseudo-friendly overtures.

The man with him had moved slightly out of earshot and Edward's expression changed as he glanced over to where his companion was studying the carved staircase, his eyes hardening as he recognised Rosy's hostility.

'Just checking out my inheritance,' he told Rosy smoothly.

'It isn't yours yet,' Rosy reminded him fiercely.

Edward gave a dismissive shrug. Unlike her father and her grandfather, Edward had run to fat in middle-age and the angry flush now mantling his face emphasised his heavy jowliness.

Her father had once remarked that Edward had a very nasty temper. On the few occasions when Rosy had met him, the tension that emanated from Edward's wife seemed to confirm her father's comment, but this was the first time she had witnessed any evidence of Edward's temper at first hand.

'Not yet, maybe, but it soon will be,' he told her angrily. 'And there's not a damn thing you or anyone else can do about it. For once in his life, the old man was too clever for his own good. How much do you reckon the staircase will fetch, Charlie?' he called out to the other man, smirking when he saw Rosy's expression.

As she watched and listened to him, any ideas Rosy might have had about appealing to his better nature died. He simply didn't have one, she recognised. He would *enjoy* destroying the house.

She heard the heavy wooden front door creak as someone pushed it open, and turned round warily, but it wasn't another of Edward's 'business associates' who had walked in, it was Guard.

He walked over to the fireplace just inside the doorway, frowning as he studied the scene in front of him.

Rosy saw the antagonism and, along with it, the apprehension flare briefly in Edward's eyes as he glared across at him, but Guard wasn't even looking at Edward, he was looking at her—looking at her, Rosy recognised in sudden, dizzy confusion, in a way she had never envisaged seeing him look at any woman, but most especially not her.

She blinked a little, her own eyes darkening as they were caught and held in a gaze of such smouldering sensuality that it actually made her physically shiver. When had Guard's eyes developed that ability to turn from cool, distant gold into hot, smouldering amber? Where had he learned to look at a woman in such a way that she and every other person in the room with her was instantly conscious of Guard's desire for her? Only Guard didn't desire her; he didn't even like her, he——

'Guard.' Rosy exclaimed weakly, her hand going automatically to her throat to protect the small pulse beating so frantically there. 'I...I didn't think you'd be back until much later.'

'I shouldn't have been,' Guard told her, 'but I couldn't bear to be away from you any longer.'

Rosy gaped at him. She could feel her skin burning. What was Guard trying to do to her? He must know as well as she did that——

She froze in shock as he crossed the hallway, dropping the briefcase he had been carrying with

a small, heavy thud as he took hold of her, holding
her so tightly against his body that she could feel
the strong bite of his fingers against her flesh; her
face was buried against his chest, any verbal response she might have wanted to make smothered,
as he murmured throatily, 'God, I've missed you.'

Rosy gulped in air nervously.

'Have you told Edward our good news yet, my
love?'

Their good news? What good news? Rosy jerked
protestingly against Guard's strong hold, lifting her
head, the impulsive words clamouring for utterance.

But she never got to say them. Instead, the swift
descent of Guard's head and the hard, totally unexpected warning pressure of his mouth on hers
stopped her.

Guard holding her. Guard kissing her. Kissing
her? Was that what he was doing? It didn't feel
much like a kiss. She opened her eyes and looked
anxiously into his. They were still that unfamiliar,
heart-thumping, pulse-racing amber colour, and the
mouth that had clamped so firmly on hers, silencing
her, somehow didn't feel anything like she might
have imagined Guard's mouth might feel if she had
ever actually allowed herself to wander into the
pitfall of such dangerous imaginings, which she
hadn't... It felt... it felt...

A dizzying wave of sensation hit her as Guard's
mouth moved slowly over hers.

Her eyes were still open and so were his, almost
hypnotising her into obeying the silent commands
he was giving her. She could feel her mouth
softening beneath the sensual impact of his, her
whole body relaxing, melting into his, relaxing and

yet at the same time being invaded by a peculiar and unfamiliar *frisson* of sensation.

To her horror, Rosy could actually feel her nipples hardening and peaking. With a small cry of protest she tore her mouth away from Guard's.

'You're right,' he agreed, as though she had spoken. 'This isn't the time or place.'

His voice sounded soft, a husky purr that made small shivers of sensation run up and down her spine. He reached out and touched her mouth with his thumb.

'What the hell's going on?'

Dizzily, Rosy dragged her gaze away from Guard's face and turned to look at Edward.

'Hasn't Rosy told you?' Guard asked politely. 'She and I are getting married. I've sorted out the special licence,' he told Rosy softly, turning away from Edward, ignoring the anger emanating from him, the questions he was asking, behaving, Rosy recognised enviously, as though Edward simply wasn't even there, as though the two of them were completely on their own, as though...

'The wedding will be just the way you wanted it to be. Very small, very quiet. In church...'

In church! Rosy tensed, but this time she managed to hold back her shocked words.

'You can't do this,' Edward was blustering angrily beside them. 'Don't think I don't know what the pair of you are up to. Don't think I won't——'

'Edward...' Without raising either his voice or his head, and still looking directly at her, Rosy marvelled, Guard had managed to silence Edward's outpourings and to get his attention. 'I think it's time you left,' Guard continued evenly. 'I'll show you out.'

Now Guard did move away from her and at another time Rosy might almost have been amused by the chagrin in Edward's expression and the confusion of his friend, who was demanding to know exactly what was going on and why Edward had brought him out on such a wild-goose chase.

'You haven't heard the last of this,' Edward warned Guard threateningly, before turning to leave. 'You aren't married yet, and besides——'

'Goodbye, Edward,' Guard interrupted him suavely, firmly closing the front door.

'Did—did you mean that?' Rosy asked him, dry-mouthed in the heavy silence that followed Edward's departure. 'About our getting married?'

'Yes,' Guard told her calmly. 'What is it, Rosy?' he asked with an abrupt return to his normal, mocking manner towards her. 'Having second thoughts?'

Rosy glanced towards the staircase and then up at the chandelier and shook her head numbly, not daring to trust her voice to make any vocal reply.

CHAPTER THREE

'DOES it have to be a church ceremony?' Rosy asked Guard uncomfortably, uncrossing her leggings-clad legs and getting up from her chair to go and stand in front of the library window.

She had been caught off-guard when he had arrived half an hour ago; nine o'clock on a Saturday morning was not exactly a time she was used to having visitors.

'Visitors?' Guard had drawled, as she had told him as much, hastily running the fingers of one hand through her tangled hair, while she surreptitiously tried to lick the small smear of jam from her toast off the fingers of the other.

In her grandfather's day, breakfast, especially at weekends, had always been a semi-formal affair, served in the breakfast-room. But, since she had been on her own, Rosy had taken to eating in the large, comfortable kitchen. Mrs Frinton, who used to come in daily to clean and cook, was now only coming in once a week. Rosy felt guilty about allowing someone to cook and clean for her when she was perfectly capable of doing both herself.

'My dear Rosy, you and I are about to be married, supposed in the eyes of the rest of the world to be desperately in love. What would seem odd to them is not so much my calling so early in the day, but the fact that I haven't stayed here all night.'

39

Predictably and irritatingly, Rosy had felt herself starting to flush.

'I have an extremely busy schedule, and there are certain things we need to discuss before the rest of the world learns our news.'

'Why should anyone else be remotely interested in what we're doing?' Rosy had demanded crossly, as Guard followed her into the library. 'Or by the rest of the world do you really mean all your girlfriends?'

The look Guard had given her had scorched her into wary silence.

Like her, Guard was dressed casually, but whereas her leggings and top shrouded the feminine shape of her body, Guard's jeans, surprisingly well-worn with tell-tale patches of lighter colour on them, clung snugly to his body, outlining the hard, taut muscles of his thighs, revealing their maleness in a way which was normally mercifully concealed by his more formal business suits.

There was, Rosy was discovering, also something almost hypnotic about the way Guard walked—about the way the denim revealed the movement of those muscles. She had been relieved when he had finally seated himself in one of the deep library chairs.

'Yes, it does,' Guard answered her original question now. 'Why the objection?'

'Well, it's just...' Rosy shrugged uncomfortably, unwilling to betray herself to his further mockery by admitting that, while she was no regular churchgoer, she felt that it was somehow wrong to marry him in church when she knew—when they *both* knew—that their marriage was simply a convenient expediency.

'Just what?' Guard pressed her.

'It's just...just that a church wedding is so much more fuss,' she fibbed lamely. 'And...'

She could feel her skin colouring under the look Guard was giving her. This morning, in the sharp, clear daylight, it seemed impossible that those clear, cold eyes could ever really have burned with that heat, that desire...that intensity she had seen last night. Nervously she looked quickly away from him. She had told herself last night, after he had gone, that that interlude—that incident—was something she was simply not going to think about. Guard had done it for Edward's benefit, and she supposed she ought to be grateful to him for going to so much trouble, but...

But it was something that most definitely must not happen again.

'Stop hedging, Rosy,' Guard told her sharply. 'You don't want to get married in church because it isn't a "real" marriage. That's typical of you and your muddled, ideological outlook on life. Try thinking things through from a more logical viewpoint. Like it or not, you and I in our different ways both have a certain standing in the local community. Edward isn't going to be happy about what we're doing, we both know that. There's no point in adding fuel to the flames of his suspicions. A small, quiet ceremony is something we can get away with—just—particularly in view of the recent deaths of your father and grandfather. Not to have a church ceremony isn't. And as for the fuss, you can leave all the arrangements to me. Which reminds

me, you'd better have a word with Mrs Frinton and
ask her if she's free to come back here to work full-
time.'

'What for?' Rosy asked him. 'I'm only using a
few of the rooms and——'

'*You* may be, but after we're married we're bound
to have to do a certain amount of entertaining. I
have business associates who'll want to be in-
troduced to my new wife, and unless you're proposing to give up your work at the shelter to be
here full time——'

Give up her work at the shelter? 'Certainly not,'
Rosy told him vehemently.

'Good. So it's agreed then. You'll contact Mrs
Frinton, tell her that we're getting married and that
I'll be moving in here and ask her——'

'You're moving in here?'

'Well, it is the normal thing for a married couple
to live under the same roof,' Guard pointed out to
her sardonically. 'Unless of course you want to
move into my apartment. Although...'

His apartment? Rosy stared at him. When Peter
had first mooted the idea of her asking Guard to
marry her, she hadn't been able to think very far
past the ordeal of actually having to propose to him.

'But we can't live together,' she began, panic
suddenly beginning to infiltrate her voice. 'We
don't...'

'We don't what? Oh, come on, Rosy... how old
are you? You can't be that naïve. You *must* have
realised when you came up with this plan of yours
to stop Edward inheriting this place that you could
hardly convince the world that this is a genuine

marriage if we're living at separate addresses. Have some sense.'

Rosy could hear the exasperation creeping into his voice.

'I hadn't really thought that far ahead,' she admitted weakly. 'I just wanted——'

'You just wanted to save the house from Edward. I know,' Guard finished for her. 'You're twenty-two years old, Rosy. Isn't it time you started to grow up?' he asked her scathingly.

'I *am* grown-up,' Rosy responded indignantly. 'I'm an adult now, Guard, a . . .'

'A what?' he asked her softly. 'A woman?'

'Yes,' she told him fiercely, her eyes darkening with anger as she saw the look he was giving her as he crossed the room.

'Turn round,' he commanded, 'and look at yourself in that mirror and tell me what you see.'

She was tempted to refuse, but the memory of how quickly and easily he had overpowered her the previous evening stopped her.

Reluctantly, instead, she did as he had demanded, staring defiantly not at her own reflection in the huge Venetian mirror over the fireplace, but at him.

How tall he looked in comparison to her own meagre height and how broad, the powerful, muscular structure of his torso clearly evident beneath the soft, checked woollen shirt he was wearing.

Her own top, in contrast, wide-necked and baggy, revealed all too clearly the vulnerable delicacy of her own bone-structure, the soft black wool somehow highlighting the translucency of her pale skin, the feminine curves of her breasts.

'A woman! You look more like a child,' Guard mocked her. 'In years you may be a woman, Rosy, but you're still hiding behind the attitude and looks of a child.' He moved in front of her, his thumb-tip rubbing briefly against her mouth, its touch gone as she instinctively lifted her hand to his wrist to push him away, her eyes dark with shock and anger.

'No lipstick,' he told her. 'No make-up of any kind.'

'It's Saturday morning,' Rosy protested. What she didn't tell him—what she couldn't tell him— was that she had overslept, that last night she had been unable to sleep because... because...

She could feel the flesh of her bottom lip prickling sensitively where he had touched it; instinctively she went to catch it between her teeth and then stopped abruptly, remembering.

'No make-up,' Guard continued remorselessly, 'clothes that hide your body, deliberately de-sexing it. Has *any* man ever seen your body, Rosy? Touched it? Touched you here?'

The fleeting touch of his hand against her breast made her tense in outraged protest, even while her body registered that there was nothing remotely sexual in his touch.

'I don't have to apologise to you or anyone else for not wanting to indulge in casual sex,' Rosy defended herself angrily. 'And just because I don't jump into bed with every male who asks me, that doesn't make me immature, or less of a woman!'

'No, it doesn't,' Guard agreed. 'But the way you blush whenever I say anything with even the re-motest sexual connotations, the way you back off from me, the way you so openly betray your inexperience sexually, *they* all say that you're not a woman, Rosy, and they'll certainly say that you're not a married woman.'

'Well, there's nothing I can do about that, is there?' Rosy snapped at him, turning away from him so that he wouldn't see either that she was blushing or that his comments had, for some odd reason, actually hurt her. 'Unless you're suggesting that I go out and find a man to go to bed with just so that I don't embarrass you with my—my lack of womanliness...'

'My God, if I thought...'

Rosy gasped as she felt Guard take hold of her, shaking her almost, and then releasing her just as abruptly, so that she didn't even have time to open her mouth to protest at his rough treatment of her. She could hear anger in his voice as he told her, 'This isn't some game we're playing, Rosy. It's re-ality—and a damn dangerous reality at that. Have you actually thought of what could happen to both of us if Edward takes it into his head to bring a case against us for fraud?'

'He wouldn't...he *couldn't* do that,' Rosy protested.

'You saw the look on his face as well as I did when he learned that he wasn't going to inherit this place,' Guard reminded her. 'One hint—just one hint that this marriage of ours is a put-up job, and he'll have his lawyers on to us so fast...'

'But he *can't* find out. He *can't* prove anything,' Rosy protested shakily.

'Not as long as we're both careful,' Guard agreed, 'and as long as you remember that you and I are now a couple. A couple who, as far as the rest of

the world are concerned, are desperately in love—
so desperately in love that they can't wait to be
together, to be married.'

Rosy gulped nervously. She had a good imagination—a very good imagination—but trying to imagine herself desperately in love with Guard . . . and
trying to imagine *him* reciprocating that love!

'Any more criticisms?' Rosy challenged him,
fighting off the feeling of panic and despair
flooding her.

The look Guard gave her made her stomach
muscles cramp nervously.

'Don't tempt me,' he advised her warningly.

Suddenly Rosy had had enough.

'You don't *have* to do this, you know,' she reminded him. 'No one's forcing you to marry me,
and I certainly don't want to marry you. Look, why
don't we just forget the whole thing, Guard?' she
exploded angrily. 'Why don't we——?'

'Why don't *you* try thinking before you open that
pretty little mouth of yours?' Guard interrupted her
savagely.

For some reason he looked even more angry now
than he had done before, Rosy realised.

'Haven't you forgotten something? Edward
knows we're supposed to be getting married.'

'So... We can pretend we've had a lovers' quarrel.
It happens all the time; you should know that,' she
told him with daring flippancy.

Oddly enough, her jibe seemed to have less effect
on him than her earlier one about their not
marrying.

'Lovers invariably make up those quarrels, at
least until they aren't lovers any longer,' Guard told

her drily. 'No, Rosy, we're committed now. It's too late for any second thoughts.'

'At least Peter was right about one thing,' Rosy told him with forced bravado. 'You must want this place one hell of a lot. You'd *have* to want something one hell of a lot to go through *this* to get it.'

She gave him a small, defeated shrug as she turned her back on him, trying to ignore the sinking, miserable sensation in the pit of her stomach as she tried not to contemplate her immediate future.

'Yes,' she heard Guard agreeing somberly. 'I would.

'I've already had a word with the vicar, by the way,' he informed her, changing the subject. 'He agreed with me that a quiet, mid-week ceremony would seem best...'

Rosy spun round.

'You've already done *what*? But...'

'*You* were the one who proposed to *me*,' Guard reminded her.

Rosy snapped her teeth together, suppressing the urge to scream. No matter what she said or did, Guard always managed to outmanoeuvre her—to outwit her.

Well, one day... One day very soon *she'd* be the one to outwit him, she promised herself and, as far as she was concerned, that day could not come fast enough.

'Did you and the vicar fix an actual date, or am I allowed to have some say in that?' Rosy asked with acid sweetness.

'Yes, a week on Wednesday,' Guard told her, ignoring her sarcasm.

'So soon? But...' Rosy gulped back her protest as she felt the cold sensation of apprehension spreading through her body.

'There's no point in delaying things,' Guard told her. 'We've only got two months to fulfil the terms of your grandfather's will. I've got several business trips coming up; in fact I'm due in Brussels again the day after the wedding, which unfortunately means that we shan't be able to have a traditional honeymoon.' When he saw Rosy's expression, he laughed sardonically. 'Yes, I thought that might appeal to you.

'The fact that we're getting married so quickly will mean that we won't need to invite many people. Neither of us has any family to speak of, and I thought we'd smooth any ruffled feathers by giving a formal reception-cum-party here later in the year. As I said, you can leave all the arrangements to me, apart from one thing. Your dress...'

'My dress?' Rosy looked at him suspiciously, guessing what was coming. 'I'm not going out and wasting money on a wedding-dress,' she warned him.

'No. So what *are* you going to wear? Not, I trust, the outfit you have on now?'

Rosy glowered at him. 'Don't be ridiculous. I'll——'

'Look, Rosy, I'm not going to waste my breath arguing with you. Your family had, and still has, a certain standing locally, which meant an awful lot to your grandfather. I appreciate that you're a modern young woman, that inherited wealth and everything that goes with it runs counter to your own beliefs, but sometimes, for the sake of other people's feelings, we have to compromise on our own principles.'

'You mean *you* want me to wear a traditional wedding-dress so that I don't let *you* down?' Rosy suggested dangerously.

'No, that is *not* what I mean.'

The anger in Guard's voice made her look directly at him. She really had annoyed him, Rosy recognised. There was a dark stain of colour angrily flushing his cheekbones and his mouth had tightened ominously. Even the way he moved, pacing restlessly from the fireplace to come and stand directly in front of her, revealed his loss of patience with her.

'*I* don't give a damn if you go to the altar wearing sackcloth and ashes, which is quite plainly what you want to wear. What is it, Rosy? Afraid that some people—someone—might not fully understand the motivation behind this marriage, that *he*—this someone—might not realise the great sacrifice you're making? Well, let me warn you now, Rosy, if you even think of telling Ralph Southern the real reason for this marriage...'

Ralph? What on earth was Guard talking about? Why should she tell Ralph anything of the sort? She already knew just how he would react if she did, just how contemptuous he would be of her desire to protect and preserve the house...

'If you think,' Guard continued grimly, 'that I——'

Rosy shook her head. Suddenly all the fight had gone out of her.

'All right, Guard. I'll wear a proper wedding-dress,' she told him woodenly, but she knew that her eyes had filled with tears and, although she tried to turn away, she wasn't quite quick enough and Guard had seen them too.

She heard him swear under his breath and then say roughly, 'All right. I'm sorry if anything I've said hurt you—but you must realise that——'

'No, it's not—it isn't anything you've said,' she said fiercely, blinking back her tears. 'I already know exactly what you think of me, Guard. It's just...' She lifted her head, unaware of how vulnerable the bravado of her stance and the resolution in her voice actually made her as she told him, 'I always imagined that when I got married...when I chose my wedding-dress...it would be——' she swallowed back the tears forming a hard lump of emotion clogging her throat '—that I'd be choosing it, *wearing* it, for a man who loved me...for a man I loved.'

She could see a small muscle beating tensely in Guard's jaw. Perhaps he was not, after all, as she had previously imagined, she recognised. Perhaps he, too, somewhere deep down inside him, had once imagined marrying for love.

'Still,' she told him, trying to appear more lighthearted than she felt, 'I suppose I can always do that the——'

'The next time,' Guard supplied harshly for her.

Rosy couldn't understand what she had said to make him so openly and furiously angry.

'I suppose you think I'm being stupid—overidealistic, naïvely romantic,' she flung at him defiantly, ignoring the instinct that told her that what she was doing was somehow dangerous. 'But I *am* romantic, Guard, and I *am* idealistic. Perhaps by the time I get to your age I might feel as you do, that loving someone and being loved by them isn't important, that it's something to sneer at and mock, but I can't help the way I feel,' she told him challengingly, lifting her head and forcing herself to make eye-contact with him, despite the nervous flutterings in her stomach. 'And just because you don't feel the same——'

'You know nothing about what I might or might not feel,' he interrupted her bitingly. 'What I may or may not have already felt or experienced ...'

Rosy could feel the wave of heat burning up over her skin as she recognised the truth of what he was saying and, with it, all that he was not saying.

Guard was an experienced, highly attractive, highly sensual man; there must have been women—or a woman—in his life to whom he had been emotionally as well as physically attracted and somehow, subtly, with his response to her own outburst, he had made her unwantedly aware of that fact.

For as long as she had known him she had felt compelled to battle and react against the air of control and authority that he exuded but now, for some reason, instead of challenging his remark, instead of asking him why if he had experienced such feelings he was still single, as she would once have done, she swallowed back that challenge.

'Let me warn you, Rosy,' she heard him saying as she turned her head away from him. 'This quest of yours to find this romantic, idealistic love isn't one that's going to be carried out whilst you're married to me. Your search for love's holy grail is one that will have to wait, I'm afraid.'

Rosy looked uncertainly at him. His comment was the kind that was normally accompanied by the mockery which always got so easily under her skin, but there was no glint of taunting humour in his eyes on this occasion, no familiar irritatingly knowing curl to his mouth.

In fact, she had rarely seen him looking so grimly serious, she recognised warily.

'For the duration of this marriage, as far as the outside world is concerned, *I* am your lover...your beloved...in every sense of those words.'

The cold flatness of his voice robbed his words of any hint of sensuality, but nevertheless Rosy could feel her skin flushing as her imagination, always her worst enemy where her run-ins with Guard were concerned, reacted to the evocative words he had used: lover, beloved. She shivered suddenly, trying to banish the images conjured up by her overactive imagination—images of two people, two lovers, their bodies entwined in an embrace of such intimacy, such compulsive desire and need for one another, that there could be no mistaking the nature of their relationship, either physically or emotionally.

Hastily, Rosy tried to banish her mental pictures, rushing into protective speech as she told Guard fiercely, 'You needn't worry. I shan't do anything to spoil your image. I mean, it just wouldn't do, would it? Guard—the fabled, famous lover— married to a woman who doesn't want him...'

'It isn't *my image*, as you call it, that concerns me,' Guard returned grimly. 'It's my professional reputation, and yours. You do realise, don't you, that technically what you and I are doing is fraudulent?' He took advantage of her wary silence to continue more easily, 'And as far as being married to a woman who doesn't want me is concerned ... You aren't a woman, Rosy, you're a girl, and I doubt that I should have much trouble finding solace elsewhere, do you...?'

For sheer arrogance there was no one like him, Rosy decided rebelliously as he turned away from her, reaching into the inside pocket of his jacket as he did so.

'You're going to need these,' he told her matter-of-factly as he handed her a small jeweller's box.

Rosy's fingers trembled slightly as she opened it, a small, totally involuntary awed gasp escaping her lips as she saw the rings inside it. The wedding-ring was plain and simple, heavy yellow gold; the engagement ring that went with it... She stared at the sapphire with its surround of dazzling, square-cut diamonds.

'It...it's beautiful,' she told Guard shakily.

The sapphire was a dense, dark blue, virtually the same colour as her own eyes, she recognised in surprise as she studied it.

'I can't wear it, Guard,' she protested huskily. 'It's...it's far too valuable.'

'You must wear it,' Guard contradicted her firmly. 'It's what people will expect—look for.'

Had he chosen the sapphire deliberately? Rosy found herself wondering. Or had it simply been a random decision, made in haste and irritation, the connection between the colour of the stone and her eyes unnoticed by him?

'Here...give me your hand.'

Reluctantly, Rosy did so, tensing slightly as he removed the ring from its box and slid it firmly down over her ring finger.

'It's...it's very beautiful,' she told Guard politely. 'Thank you.'

'Is that the best you can do? You sound like a child thanking an adult for some extra pocket money. It *is* customary to thank one's prospective bridegroom in a rather more intimate fashion for such a gift.'

His glance dropped to her mouth as he spoke, and Rosy was irritated by the wave of self-consciousness that swept over her. He was doing it deliberately, of course. Well, she'd show him. Gritting her teeth, she lifted her face obediently towards his, instinctively closing her eyes as she waited ... and waited.

When nothing happened, she opened her eyes and glared angrily at Guard.

'If that's the best you can do, then the more of this marriage of ours that's conducted out of public view, the better,' Guard told her cynically. 'For your information, my dear Rosy, a newly engaged, supposedly ecstatically in love woman does not screw up her face and react to the thought of being kissed by her fiancé as though she's been told she has to take a dose of medicine.'

'But we aren't ecstatically in love,' Rosy reminded him crossly.

'And for all the reasons I've already been through with you, it is extremely important that no one else other than us knows that,' Guard pointed out. 'Edward isn't a fool, Rosy,' he warned her. 'If he thinks he's got the slightest chance of disputing your claim to this place, he's going to take it.'

'So what am I supposed to do?' Rosy demanded defensively. 'Take lessons in how to kiss a man as though I love him when I don't? No, thanks, I don't need them,' she snapped.

'No? That's not the impression I got. A kiss between two committed lovers is nothing like the jumbled, bungled efforts you've obviously experienced,' Guard told her.

Rosy glared furiously back at him, caught between anger and embarrassment. She wanted to tell Guard that she knew exactly what it felt like to exchange wildly passionate kisses with a man she wanted, but she was uncomfortably aware that it simply wasn't true.

The kisses and the men she had known so far had all left her depressingly unmoved.

'I'm not an actress, Guard,' she told him more cautiously instead. 'I can't manufacture passion to order...'

'No?' Guard commented softly. 'Then perhaps it's time you learned.'

He was still holding her hand; holding her hand and standing so close to her that all he had to do to close the gap between them was simply to take a single step towards her.

Rosy tensed as she waited for him to imprison her in his arms, knowing he was far too strong for her to be able to break free; but instead he slowly lifted his free hand and gently brushed her hair back off her face.

'This is how a man deeply in love touches a woman, Rosy,' he told her quietly. 'She seems so vulnerable, so delicate, so precious to him that he's half afraid to touch her, half afraid that the merest sensation of her skin against his fingertips will ignite a passion within him that he simply cannot control. He wants her...her wants her desperately and overpoweringly, and yet at the same time he wants to go oh, so slowly with her, to savour and hold on to every millisecond of contact with her.

'He is caught between those twin needs—his hunger for her, his urgent desire to possess and devour her, and his desire to worship her, to give her all the pleasure he can...all the pleasure there is. And so he touches her skin, gently and perhaps even a little unsteadily and, as he does so, he looks into her eyes, wanting to see in them that his passion, his need, his *love* are reciprocated, wanting to see that she *knows* and understands how great the strain of his self-imposed self-control is.

'If she does return his feelings, she, too, will reach out and touch him.'

Mesmerised by the soft timbre of Guard's words, Rosy didn't even blink as he lifted her left hand to his jaw.

Freed momentarily from the hypnotism of his eyes, she flinched a little beneath the sharp quiver of unexpected sensation that ran through her body as her fingertips touched the slight roughness of Guard's jaw.

He had turned his head away from her and she gasped out aloud as she felt his lips caressing the soft centre of her palm and then the inside of her wrist where her pulse was beating so fast that its frantic race was making her feel quite dizzy.

'A man in love will take his time in reaching his ultimate target,' Guard was telling her softly. 'He'll kiss her throat, her ears...'

Rosy trembled as she felt the soft brush of Guard's mouth against her skin.

'But all the time what he really wants...'

Rosy tensed as she felt the warmth of Guard's breath moving across her face. Her mouth had gone apprehensively dry, her lips parting a little in her need to draw extra air into her lungs.

'Her mouth will draw him like a magnet...lure him, make him ache from head to foot in his need to taste its velvet softness—to taste *her*, to possess her in what is in reality a sensual preparation and stimulant, a taste of what is to come when they enjoy a far more intimate exploration of one another.

'When a man in love kisses a woman's mouth and explores the taste of her already, in his mind, in his *body*, he is imagining—anticipating—the far more intimate taste of her.'

Rosy shivered. She was drowning in a flood of consuming heat caused by what she told herself was fury and embarrassment at what Guard was doing...saying to her.

She could feel the warmth of his breath against her lips, the heat of his palm against her scalp beneath her hair as he supported her head with one hand; the other was slowly caressing her back, stroking dangerously along her spine.

'He kisses her gently at first,' Guard told her. 'Like this...'

The pressure of his mouth against hers, so light that it was barely there at all, should surely not be having such a traumatic effect on her, Rosy fretted anxiously. It was sheer instinct, her desire to get what was, after all, an extremely uncomfortable and embarrassing episode well and truly behind her, that was making her want to press her mouth more urgently against Guard's.

'And then, as his need for her overwhelms him, like this...'

Rosy gasped in protest as the pressure of Guard's mouth on hers changed and hardened so quickly and devastatingly that shock paralysed her.

So this, then, was the way a man kissed, the way his mouth moved with hard urgency on yours, Rosy thought dizzily, the way the embrace involved not just the pressure of his mouth on your own but the whole of his body...and the whole of yours as well.

She was trembling, Rosy recognised, trembling helplessly, overwhelmed by her awareness of the vast gulf which lay between Guard's sexual experience and her own.

And the shock of that knowledge was somehow like a physical pain, aching through her body, making her eyes sting with sharp tears.

When the pressure of Guard's mouth against her own eased, she felt almost sick with relief, until she realised that he wasn't going to release her at all— that he was——

'Open your mouth, Rosy,' he instructed her. 'Only children kiss with their mouths closed, or didn't you know that?'

'Of course I know,' she snapped indignantly, stiffening in outrage as Guard refused to let her continue, covering her mouth with his own, drawing the breath from her as he demonstrated what he had just been telling her.

Rosy had exchanged such kisses with boys before, exchanged them and felt mildly saddened because she was not feeling the almost mystical intense passion and sense of intimacy she had expected to feel.

But with Guard it was different... With Guard...

She could feel herself starting to tremble convulsively as her body registered its awareness of what was happening.

Confused, bewildered thoughts tumbled headlong through her brain as she tried to comprehend why it was that Guard's mouth... Guard's kiss... Guard's manufactured and totally fictitious passion should have the power to deceive her senses into believing... wanting...

With a small, frantic cry, she jerked back from him. She had never seen Guard's eyes look so... so...

She flinched as he reached out and touched her bottom lip with his thumb, demanding raggedly, 'Don't...'

'Turn round,' Guard told her.

Unwillingly she did so.

'Now look in the mirror.'

Guard was standing behind her, his hands resting lightly on her shoulders, his face unreadable as Rosy focused unwillingly on their reflections.

'When a woman's been thoroughly kissed... *properly* kissed,' Guard told her quietly, 'it shows here...'

Rosy tensed as he reached out and touched the swollen fullness of her mouth, her eyes immediately darkening in response to his touch.

'And if she's particularly sensitive and responsive,' Guard continued calmly, 'it even shows here as well.'

The clinical detachment with which he so accurately traced a circle around the areola of her nipple took Rosy's breath away so completely that she was unable to utter any kind of protest.

Because of her thick sweater it was impossible for him to see—to *know*—how her nipples had swelled and hardened when he kissed her. Totally and completely impossible.

And there was certainly nothing in his clinical detachment to suggest that he did know, Rosy reflected with feverish relief as he released her and stood back from her.

Even so, she could still feel the hot, self-conscious colour sweeping up over her body despite her efforts to suppress it.

She struggled to think of something to say—some throw-away, casual remark to make—but her brain refused to supply one, her thought processes reduced to a thick, immobilising, treacle-like sludge.

As Guard turned away from her to walk towards the door, she found herself wondering silently how many women there had been in his life who had generated the reality of the passion he had manufactured to show her.

As he reached the door, he turned back towards her, warning her, 'It's too late to change your mind now, Rosy.'

CHAPTER FOUR

'YOU'RE doing what?'

There was no mistaking the shock nor the anger in Ralph's voice, Rosy recognised unhappily.

It had taken her over a week to bring herself to the point of telling Ralph about her marriage. Not because she had anticipated his reaction—she hadn't—but because she had been afraid that he would guess the truth.

Peter, as well as Guard, had warned her of the dangerous position she could put herself in if people started suspecting that her marriage was simply a ploy to keep the house.

'You and I may know how altruistic your motives are,' Peter had told her, 'but others may not.'

'Guard says that Edward could bring a case for fraud against us,' Rosy had told him. 'Is that true?'

'It's a possibility,' Peter had agreed cautiously. 'But he would have to have strong, almost irrefutable proof that the marriage was sham in order to do that. To be able to prove, for instance, that there was quite definitely no possibility of the marriage producing a child...'

'But there isn't,' Rosy had told him quickly. 'You know——'

'*I* know, *you* know and *Guard* knows,' Peter had anticipated her, 'but no one else knows—nor must anyone else know.'

And so Rosy had put off telling Ralph about her marriage, afraid that she might not be able to play her role of deliriously-in-love bride-to-be adequately enough to deceive him.

In the end, though, it wasn't her lack of love for Guard he had questioned, but Guard's for her.

'For God's sake, Rosy, don't you *see* what he's after?' Ralph demanded. 'He wants the one thing that he knows his money has never and will never be able to buy.'

'You mean me?' Rosy quipped.

'No, I don't. I mean Queen's Meadow,' Ralph told her grimly. 'It's no secret that he's always wanted the house. Your grandfather refused to sell it to him.'

'Guard and I love each other, Ralph,' Rosy interrupted him, superstitiously crossing her fingers in the folds of her skirt as she did so, glad that Ralph was looking directly at her as she told the lie.

'Oh, Rosy...can't you see? Men like Guard don't fall in love with——'

He broke off, his thin, slightly foxy face flushing slightly. 'Look, I don't want to hurt you, Rosy. You're an attractive girl—a very attractive girl— but in terms of...of experience, you and Guard might almost have come from different planets.

'You've seen here at the shelter the havoc that unbalanced relationships can cause, the pain that comes from an unequal relationship. Can you honestly tell me that you and Guard are equals in every way; that you and he...?'

'We're in love, Ralph,' Rosy repeated. 'And——'

'And he'll teach you everything you need to know. Both in bed and out of it. Rubbish,' Ralph told her. 'If you really, honestly believe that, then you're not the person I took you for. Sure, he'll enjoy playing with you for a few weeks—a few months possibly—but after that... Don't go through with it, Rosy. You don't need to marry him. You——'

'Yes, I do.'

The quiet, sad admission was made before Rosy could help herself, the words spoken so softly under her breath that Ralph couldn't hear them.

She looked up as the office door burst open and a woman, accompanied by two small children, came rushing in demanding to speak to Ralph.

Liz Phillips was one of their regulars at the shelter, periodically leaving her violent husband, announcing that there was no power on earth that could ever make her go back again, only to do exactly that within weeks of having left him.

'She must love him so much,' Rosy had commented innocently when she had first started working at the shelter.

'Yeah, like an alcoholic loves his drink, an addict his next fix; she's addicted to him, to the violence of their relationship,' Ralph had told her grimly. 'A part of her needs and craves what she sees as the excitement and uncertainty of their relationship. But for every Liz Phillips we get here, we get a hundred women who do genuinely want to break away from their relationship and start again, who need us to help them to make that break.'

'How do you recognise the difference?' Rosy had asked in bewilderment.

'With experience,' Ralph had told her shortly. 'Like everything else.'

Then, she had thought that Ralph was being unfairly hard. Now she knew better but, for once, as she finished her work, it was not the concerns of the shelter and its inmates that were absorbing her, but her own worries.

Guard had not looked too pleased when she had told him she wanted to invite Ralph to their wedding, but Rosy had remained adamant that she wanted him there.

Peter was giving her away. Guard had drafted a notice to be put in the Press, announcing their marriage; only a handful of people had been invited to the actual ceremony.

The ceremony. In two days' time she and Guard would be married. Husband and wife. It was a situation her imagination could still not encompass. She and Guard...husband and wife...Mr and Mrs... She and Guard participating in a deception which, if it was ever discovered...

Did all brides feel like this? Rosy wondered nervously as the car stopped outside the church and Peter got out. Or were her hands icy-cold, her mind and emotions frozen and numb simply because of the circumstances surrounding her particular marriage?

This morning, putting on her wedding-dress, standing stiffly in front of the mirror while Mrs Frinton fussed over her, fastening the hundred and one tiny satin-covered buttons that ran from the nape of her neck right down under the bustle and bow that ornamented the back of her dress, she had felt such anguish and guilt, such pain, that she had been tempted to tear off the dress and simply walk away... disappear. But then Peter had arrived and with him the flowers Guard had sent her, and events had developed a momentum it was impossible for her to resist.

And now here she was, walking into the lofty parish church, past the stained-glass window donated by one of her ancestors. The ivory satin of the wedding-dress, which had been her mother's and was a Dior original into which she had still had to squeeze herself—despite the weight she had lost this last week—so tiny had been her mother's waist, still had, clinging to its folds, a faint hint of the perfume Rosy could remember her mother wearing. Wearing it made her feel as though she was carrying a little of her mother with her.

That knowledge brought hot tears to her eyes which she fiercely blinked back.

The veil, once white but now ivory with age, had been her great-grandmother's. In wearing garments which had originally been worn with love, she felt as though she were somehow compensating for the lack of emotion in her own marriage.

Marriage. It *wasn't* a marriage, she reminded herself starkly. It was a business arrangement, that was all. A contract...

The church felt cold, the stone slabs beneath her feet striking icy-cold through the thin soles of her shoes.

The church was bleakly empty, only the first two pews filled. Someone, Guard presumably, had arranged for the hugely extravagant cream and white floral decorations which warmed the cold, austere dimness of the building.

As she saw Guard for the first time Rosy's footsteps faltered slightly and, even though he could not possibly have heard the soft, distressed sound she suppressed, he turned round.

He looked so remote and distant. It seemed impossible to imagine that she was actually marrying him. Rosy shivered, glad of the protection of her veil to hide her expression from him.

'Edward's watching you,' Peter warned her. 'Smile.'

Edward. Rosy hadn't even realised he was in church, but now she could see him, and with him his wife and his sons—two pale, subdued copies of their mother, hair slicked back, school uniforms on. Rosy flinched slightly as she looked hurriedly away from the taller of the pair.

By her marriage to Guard she was depriving him of his opportunity to inherit Queen's Meadow. Only, if Edward inherited, there would no longer be a Queen's Meadow for him to inherit.

She clung to that knowledge for comfort as she finally reached Guard's side.

The raucous, inappropriately joyful peal of the bells was making her feel sick, Rosy acknowledged as she blinked in the sharp clarity of the sunlight. Or was it the shock of that moment when Guard had thrown back her veil and looked so deeply into her eyes as the vicar pronounced them husband and wife that, for a fraction of time, even she had almost been deceived that the emotion, the intensity, the passion which had darkened his eyes as he looked into hers had been real.

There were people milling all around her. Where had they come from? Dizzily she recognised some of the women from the shelter, people who had known her father and grandfather, all of them smiling, laughing, making teasing comments about the suddenness of her marriage. All of them apart from Edward.

Rosy tensed as she saw the malevolence in his eyes.

She had always known he didn't like her, but it had never worried her. *She* did not like *him*, but now she recognised his dislike was different. Now she was standing between him and what he coveted, what he had assumed would be his.

A small shiver ran over her.

'What is it, what's wrong?'

Rosy tensed in surprise at Guard's question. She hadn't expected him to notice her small, betraying *frisson* of apprehension. He had appeared to be deep in conversation with Peter, too deeply involved to be aware of her.

'Nothing,' she told him guardedly, aware that Edward was still watching her, watching them both.

'That's a beautiful dress,' someone commented to her.

'Thank you. It was my mother's,' she responded absently.

'I thought I recognised it.'

That was Guard, catching her unaware for a second time, making her mouth open in a small 'O' of astonishment as she turned to face him.

'Your father had a photograph of her wearing it on his desk,' Guard reminded her. 'It suits you. The colour complements your skin. It has the same warm tint...'

He reached out and brushed his fingers lightly against her throat as he spoke.

'Edward's watching us,' Rosy warned him in a small, stifled voice.

'Yes. I know.'

'Do you think he suspects?' Rosy asked him nervously.

'If he does, this should stop him,' Guard assured her.

'This...?' Rosy looked up at him questioningly and then went still as she recognised the slow accomplished movements of his body, performed like some magical sleight of hand so that, to their onlookers, it must seem as though the way he took her in his arms, the way he held and kissed her, were the actions of a man so deeply in love with his bride that not even their discreetly curious observation could prevent him from exhibiting his feelings.

Unexpectedly, behind her closed eyelids, she could feel the hot burn of tears.

This was no time to go stupidly sentimental, she warned herself shakily. No time to compare the emotions her mother must have felt when she wore this dress to her own——

'Oh, I think it's all so romantic,' Edward's wife sighed enviously, as Guard released Rosy. 'It's just such a shame that your father...'

'John knew how I feel about Rosy,' Rosy heard Guard saying calmly.

He certainly had, Rosy acknowledged, but not in the way that Guard was implying. She could well remember her father once making an idle and half-envious comment about Guard being able to have any woman he wanted.

Rosy had been just seventeen then and she had reacted accordingly.

'He couldn't have me,' she had told her father challengingly.

Her father had laughed.

'You aren't a woman yet, poppet, and I doubt very much that Guard would *want* you anyway. He knows you far too well... what a little shrew you can be at times...'

'Where are you going for your honeymoon? Or aren't we allowed to ask?' Rosy heard Edward enquiring.

'We aren't,' Guard replied for her. 'At least not yet. I have a meeting in Brussels in two days' time which I couldn't put off. Rosy and I fly out there tomorrow morning.'

They flew out there? Rosy stared at him, but Guard was looking in the opposite direction, answering some comment that the vicar's wife had made to him, and Rosy had to wait until they were alone in the bridal car to ask him uneasily, 'Why did you tell Edward that we're both going to Brussels? He's bound to suspect something if he discovers that I haven't gone.'

She whispered the question, even though the glass panel between them and the driver was closed. That was what deceit did to you, she recognised mournfully. It made you cautious... wary... *guilty*.

'There won't be anything for him to discover,' Guard told her promptly. 'I meant what I said.'

'You mean you're expecting me to go to Brussels with you—without even asking me?' Rosy demanded indignantly. 'But I can't—I'm supposed to be working at the shelter...'

'Don't be ridiculous, Rosy,' Guard told her dampeningly. 'Dedicated though he is, Ralph is hardly likely to expect you to go back to work quite so quickly.'

'But I want to,' Rosy told him aggressively.

'If you do, you'll be putting us both at risk,' Guard warned her. 'It takes more than a church service to make a marriage, Rosy.'

Angrily, Rosy turned her head away from him. She knew full well what it took to make a marriage, but their marriage wasn't going to include *that* particular ingredient, and Guard knew it.

'It takes,' Guard continued calmly, 'a degree of intimacy which *most* couples develop in bed, but which you and I will have to find another way to manufacture. We need some time on our own to establish ourselves in our new roles, Rosy...'

When she didn't respond, he continued inexorably, '*You* were the one who wanted this marriage——'

'To save the house,' Rosy interrupted him angrily. 'Not because...'

In her heart of hearts she knew that Guard was right that the awkwardness she felt when she was with him was bound to betray her, but the last thing she wanted to do was to spend time on her own with him. In her view, that would only exacerbate the problem, not solve it.

'I don't want to go away with you, Guard,' she told him dangerously now. 'I don't want to come back and have people looking at us...speculating...imagining...believing...'

'What?' he challenged her, his eyebrows lifting.

'You know what,' Rosy muttered, avoiding looking directly at him.

'Thinking that we've been to bed together? Most of them assume that we've already done that. Imagining that we've spent the whole of the time we've been away making love...that my supposed business meeting is just a fiction and that in reality the hours I should have spent seated behind some boardroom table have been spent exploring every inch of your body, stroking and caressing it until I know every contour of it, every hollow and curve.'

Out of the corner of her eye Rosy could see the way his glance was lingering on her breasts and immediately the hot, agitated colour flared in her face.

'Such embarrassment,' Guard mocked her. 'You'd burn with that colour from the tip of your toes to the top of your head if I told you exactly what I'd expect and want the woman I loved to do to my body the first time we went to bed together,' Guard told her outrageously. 'Have you ever even *seen* a naked man, Rosy? Never mind——'

'Of course I have,' she lied hotly, interrupting him. 'I realise how much you like making fun of me, Guard,' she added with angry dignity. 'Yes, I do get...embarrassed when you talk about such—such intimate things. And no, my experience doesn't come anywhere near matching yours but, contrary to what you seem to believe, I *prefer* to be the way I am. *Anyone* can get sexual experience,' she added, gathering confidence when he didn't make any attempt to interrupt her or mock her. 'And just because I choose *not* to do so——'

'Just as a matter of interest, Rosy, *why* have you chosen not to do so?'

'You *know* why,' Rosy told him huskily.

'Because you're saving yourself for the man of your dreams,' Guard mocked her. 'What happens if you never meet him, Rosy? Have you ever asked yourself that?' Guard demanded with such unexpected savagery in his voice that his anger shocked her.

CHAPTER FIVE

'BUT this isn't a hotel,' Rosy protested as Guard swung their hired car up the drive and stopped in front of the entrance to an impressive, stone-built château.

Ever since Guard had made his announcement that she was going to Brussels with him Rosy had protested and argued that she didn't want to, but it hadn't made any difference.

'And what am I supposed to do,' she had exploded angrily, 'while you're in your meetings?'

'You've never struck me as a person so uninterested in her fellow human beings that she suffers from boredom, Rosy, far from it...'

Rosy had glared suspiciously at him. Compliments from Guard? He must have some ulterior motive, and she suspected she knew quite well what it was. She wasn't a complete fool.

'I'm not going with you, Guard,' she had told him. 'I don't *want* to go with you.'

But, somehow or other, all her protests had been overruled and now here she was, glaring frustratedly at Guard's profile, thoroughly incensed by his ability to remain calm when all her emotions were a seething mass of churning chaos.

She wasn't used to being married; she wasn't used to having a husband, to being part of a pair... a couple, and she resented Guard's apparent assumption that *he* should be the one to decide what they should and should not do—what she should and should not do.

'No, it isn't a hotel,' he responded calmly now. 'It's a private home. Madame, the châtelaine, is French and, rather than sell the property after her husband's death, she decided to supplement her income by taking in paying guests. Like most Frenchwomen, she is not just an excellent cook, but a first-rate hostess and extremely skilled in the art of making one comfortable.'

Rosy frowned. Something in Guard's voice when he spoke about the owner of the château irked her a little. Without his having described her in any detail, Rosy immediately had a mental image of one of those elegant, ageless Frenchwomen whom she, personally, had always found particularly intimidating.

'But you said you had business in *Brussels*,' she objected. 'This place is miles away.'

'A little over two hours' drive,' Guard told her. 'That's all. And staying here gives me an excuse not to get involved in the Brussels political scene, which can be as pedantic as the people involved in it. I thought you'd like it here. You've always said you prefer the country to the city.'

Rosy looked away from him. It was true that she *did* prefer the country, and normally she would probably have enjoyed such a trip, but normally she would not have been making it with Guard—as his wife.

Guard was already climbing out of the car and going round to open her door.

Unwillingly, she had exchanged her normal favourite wear of leggings and a comfortable top

for a long jersey skirt with a matching waistcoat.
Beneath it she was wearing a soft, cream shirt. The
outfit had a matching knitted jacket which she had
brought with her just in case she felt cold.

She had worn the outfit knowing that it wasn't
likely to crease, a fact of which she was uncharac-
teristically glad as the door of the château opened
and Guard's Frenchwoman appeared.

Predictably, she was dressed in black—a wool,
crêpe skirt which Rosy suspected must have come
from one of the couture houses, teamed with a plain
satin shirt and a cashmere knit draped flatteringly
round her shoulders. The pearls gleaming at her
throat—all three rich ropes of them—had to be real,
just like the diamonds on her fingers and in her
ears, but it wasn't her elegance that struck Rosy as
she reluctantly fell into step beside Guard, it was
her age, or rather her lack of it.

The woman was not, as she had expected, somewhere in her late fifties or early sixties, but far closer
to forty—closer, in fact, to Guard in age than she
was herself, Rosy recognised.

Quite why that knowledge should cause her to
feel so hostile towards Madame, she had no idea,
but that she was not alone in that feeling became
quite clear.

Madame turned to Guard, totally ignoring Rosy,
to say coolly to him, 'Oh, I hadn't realised that you
would be bringing a . . . friend with you.'

'Rosy is my wife,' Guard explained firmly,
drawing Rosy forward and introducing her.

Friend or wife, it plainly made no difference as
far as Madame was concerned; she was obviously
not pleased about Rosy's presence.

'I had put you in your normal suite,' she told
Guard, somehow or other managing to stand in between them so that she was facing Guard but had
her back to *her*, Rosy observed, as she listened to
the Frenchwoman speaking to Guard in her own
tongue.

Rosy's own French was extremely fluent. She had
a gift for languages which had been fostered during
the years her father had been stationed in Germany.
Her French was, in fact, far more fluent than
Guard's.

'However, if you should prefer another room...'
Madame was saying.

Another room. Rosy's heart thumped
uncomfortably.

She had assumed that they would be staying in
Brussels in a large, anonymous hotel and that they
would, as a matter of course, have separate rooms.
After all, Guard could have as little desire to share
the intimacy of a bedroom as she did.

'No, my usual suite will be fine,' Guard was as-
suring their hostess.

The large, draughty hallway of the château made
Rosy glad of her long skirt.

Queen's Meadow was kept relatively warm by its
low ceilings and thick panelling, but this place, with
its lofty rooms and bare stone walls, must be a
nightmare to heat, Rosy reflected as Madame
preceded them up the stone staircase.

Its carpet, although well-worn, was decorated
with what Rosy presumed were the arms of her late
husband's family. Rosy paused to examine them
more closely, wondering if she was correct in in-
terpreting that the bend sinister in one quarter of

it with the fleur-de-lys meant that at some point in history one of the château's châtelaines had been a Royal mistress and had borne her lover a son.

Up ahead of her, Madame was walking side by side with Guard, saying something in French about regretting the fact that his wife's presence meant that they would not have their normal tête-à-tête dinner together.

Guard's urbane and English, 'No, I'm afraid not, but I'm sure that Rosy will thoroughly enjoy sampling your wonderful culinary skills,' made Rosy glower at him. There was surely no need for him to practise his role of supposedly loving husband *here*.

It was on the tip of her tongue to say that, as far as she was concerned, he and Madame could enjoy as many tête-à-têtes as they wished, but instead she suppressed the impulse, contenting herself with a less-than-warm smile in Madame's direction and telling her in her own fluent French that she was indeed thoroughly looking forward to such a treat.

Apart from a narrow-eyed look and a faint pursing of her artfully carmined mouth, Madame made no comment. But she was no longer talking to Guard in French, Rosy noticed, as the older woman walked them along a corridor, stopping outside a heavy, wooden door.

'I trust everything will be to your liking,' she told Rosy formally and without conviction.

This time it was Rosy's turn to be distantly unresponsive.

As the woman left them the thought crossed her mind that the relationship between her and Guard could have been far more intimate than that of

hostess and guest but, oddly for her, it was a suspicion that she didn't voice.

Her impetuosity had always been something of
a joke in the family, and she was ruefully aware
that she did have a tendency to speak before she
thought, but when it came to Guard's personal life,
and his sexual experience, it wasn't just reticence
that held her back.

Just thinking about Guard and sex made her
stomach clench nervously and her body grow hot
and wary. There was, she admitted, something
simply far too dangerous about the whole subject
for her to risk making any kind of unguarded
comment about it, to risk giving Guard the opportunity to taunt her about her own comparative
innocence and ignorance.

And yet with other men she felt no such discomfort—quite the opposite. As she walked past
Guard and into the suite's sitting-room she was immediately aware of the scent of Madame's perfume,
lingering on the air. Silently, she studied her sur-
roundings—the giltwood furniture, the hugely
ornate gilded mirror above the fireplace, the rococo
work and the silk wall-hangings in a pale green
moire that seemed to shimmer with a life of its own.

Vases of white, waxy lilies added to the room's
elegance; it would have been easy to find such a
setting quite intimidating, Rosy recognised as she
frowned down at the faded Aubusson rug on the
floor.

'I normally use this bedroom,' she heard Guard
saying from behind her as he opened one of the
two doors leading out of the room. 'It has an ad-

joining bathroom; the other one does not, but if you'd prefer...'

What she'd prefer would be to be at home, on her own, Rosy recognised grimly, as Guard well knew.

'I don't care,' she told him dismissively and then couldn't resist adding, 'Hadn't you better have the one with the bathroom? After all, I'm sure Madame will expect you to be properly groomed before you join her for your usual tête-à-tête.'

'Jealous?'

The soft taunt, so unexpected and so impossible, shocked her into silence.

Jealous... How could she be? Guard meant nothing to her. The only emotions that existed between them were a dismissive contempt for her on his part, and an impotent antagonism towards him on hers.

Jealous... It was impossible, unthinkable, and Guard knew it. So why had he said it?

She shook her head, unable to bring herself to make the denial. Why should she when there was nothing to deny?

Instead, she turned her head away from him and reminded him fiercely, 'I didn't want to come here, Guard.'

'Maybe not, but you are here. *We* are here, and while we're here——'

As she started to walk away from him, he moved towards her, barring her way to the bedroom door.

'Look at me, Rosy,' he commanded. 'You aren't a child any more, to be indulged by being allowed to walk away from an argument to save face when you know you can't win it.'

'An argument?' Rosy gave him a bitter look. 'When has anyone ever been *allowed* to argue with you, Guard? I thought you were omnipotent—all-seeing, all-knowing. So...go on... While we're here, what? I can sit like an obedient child playing gooseberry whilst you and Madame——'

'There is nothing between Madame la Comtesse and me,' Guard told her grimly, emphasising the older woman's title.

'Maybe not, but *she* would like there to be,' Rosy guessed intuitively.

'I repeat, there is nothing between us,' Guard continued, ignoring Rosy's comment. 'But even if there were...'

'It would be none of my business,' Rosy supplied sarcastically.

'Perhaps not,' Guard agreed levelly. 'But that was not what I was going to say. What I was going to say, Rosy, was that you should at least try to put your antagonism towards me to one side occasionally and apply the laws of logic and rationality, instead of giving way to those over-imaginative emotions of yours.

'The reason I insisted that you come with me on this trip was to give us both time to adjust to our new...status. To have done that and then brought you into the presence of my lover would hardly make much sense, would it?

'The time to worry, my dear, is not when I insist on your accompanying me on business trips, but when I start making excuses *not* to take you.'

For some reason he was smiling, a fact which infuriated Rosy so much that she could feel her face starting to burn with angry colour.

'So much passion and so little outlet for it,' Guard mocked her, touching one hot cheek with a cool fingertip.

'Stop patronising me, Guard,' Rosy demanded heatedly. 'I'm not a child.'

'No?' The smile disappeared, to be replaced by an assessingly level look. 'If only that were true.'

'No, thank you. No more wine for me,' Rosy refused, shaking her head and valiantly trying to suppress a yawn.

Guard had not exaggerated Madame's culinary talents, but Rosy had not really enjoyed the meal. The way Madame had deliberately excluded her from the conversation and concentrated exclusively on Guard had at first amused and then later irked her.

To be fair, she had to admit that Guard had done his best to reverse Madame's bad manners, making a point of bringing Rosy into their discussions, but Rosy had grown tired of the game and longed to make her excuses and escape to her bed.

'In fact, if you don't mind, I think I'll go to bed,' she added quietly, standing up before Guard could say anything and formally thanking their hostess, and complimenting her on the meal.

Guard's quiet and totally unexpected, 'I think I'll come with you,' shocked her into protesting.

'No, you stay here.' But Guard was already slipping his hand under her elbow and adding his thanks to hers as he walked with her to the door.

'You didn't have to do that,' Rosy snapped once they were in the hallway. 'You could have stayed.'

'What, and leave my new bride on her own?' Guard drawled mockingly.

Rosy glowered at him, compressing her lips.

'There's no need to be so sarcastic,' she told him crossly. 'I'm not a complete fool, Guard. I know quite well that you——'

When she stopped, he prompted, 'That I what?' But Rosy refused to be drawn, shaking her head. What was the point in saying what they both knew? That she was the last person that Guard would want to marry—and the last person to want to marry *him*?

'I don't know why you brought me here,' she repeated untruthfully, her temper suddenly exploding. 'What am *I* supposed to do with myself while you're in Brussels. Ask Madame to give me some cooking tips?'

'You won't be staying here,' Guard told her promptly. 'You're coming with me.'

'What?' Rosy stared at him.

'I think you'll find Monsieur Dubois rather interesting and, since he doesn't speak English and my French is rather on the pedestrian side, I'd certainly appreciate your assistance.'

What did Guard mean? She'd find Monsieur Dubois interesting? Guard's business involved providing extremely detailed and complex computer programs, a subject about which Rosy knew very little, as Guard well knew.

'Monsieur Dubois is a keen environmentalist,' Guard continued, correctly reading her mind. 'He is the spokesperson for a very influential group lobbying the EEC for better and tighter controls over the destruction of the natural vegetation of the countryside and, since that's something I know you take a keen interest in, you should have a lot in common.'

It was so unlike Guard to make a comment to her that did not include mockery of one sort or another that for once Rosy could think of nothing to say.

'And, of course, having you to translate for me will save me the cost of hiring an interpreter,' Guard added.

Rosy flashed him an indignant look. Just for a second she had almost been deceived into thinking that for once he was treating her as an equal, an adult. She was so irritated that she was almost tempted to refuse to go with him, but the alternative of staying at the château was not an appealing one.

'I've got some notes I need to read up,' Guard told her as he unlocked their suite door, 'so if you want to use the bathroom first...'

Rosy knew she ought to feel grateful to him for his tact, but instead she felt ruffled and awkward, like a child sent to bed to be out of the way of the adults. Was Guard's claim that he wanted to do some work simply a ruse to get rid of her so that he could go back downstairs to rejoin Madame?

If Guard wanted to be with the Frenchwoman, then he had no need to lie to her, Rosy decided angrily. He was a perfectly free agent in *that* respect; they both were.

So why did the thought of Guard and Madame, their dark heads close together while Madame's scarlet, pouting mouth whispered in Guard's ear, cause her such an uncomfortable and unpleasant sensation in the pit of her stomach?

Its cause, Rosy decided, thoroughly disgruntled, was surely not so much an emotional reaction to the thought of Madame's overpainted, full red mouth against Guard's ear, but rather a physical reaction to the reality of Madame's over-rich food in her stomach!

When she had first agreed with Peter to try to save the house she had not fully realised exactly what she was letting herself in for, she admitted bleakly as she undressed and stepped into the huge, claw-footed bath. The last couple of weeks had been far more stressful than she had expected—than she wanted to admit.

There had been a moment at the wedding breakfast when she had looked at the familiar faces around her and suddenly and sharply ached for the comforting and familiar presence of her father and grandfather.

Mortified by her own weakness and the tears which had filled her eyes and choked her throat, she had quickly bent her head over her plate, hoping that no one had noticed. Guard had been safely engaged in conversation with Edward's wife, or so she had thought, which had made it even more humiliating when he had pushed a large, clean handkerchief into her hand and told her quietly, 'I miss them too, Rosy. That at least is something that we do share.'

Unexpectedly, tears filled her eyes now. Crossly she blinked them away. What was the matter with her these days? She had never been the crying type.

Madame might be generous with her food, but she was mean with her hot water, Rosy decided as she washed herself quickly and jumped out of the bath, wrapping herself in a thick, white towel and then rubbing her body briskly with it—as much to banish her too-intrusive memories as to dry her skin.

As she pulled on her cotton T-shirt, with its cartoon drawings on the front, she grimaced at her reflection in the bathroom mirror.

No one seeing her now would ever be deceived into believing she was a rapturously happy bride, she acknowledged.

When and if Guard did marry, she doubted that it would be to a woman—a *girl*—who wore cotton T-shirts to bed and plain white underwear. She doubted that Madame, for instance, even possessed such garments.

Picking up her discarded clothes, she headed for the bedroom, calling out as she entered it, 'Guard, I've finished in the bathroom now.'

Silence. Had he heard her? She frowned, nibbling at her bottom lip as she stared at the closed bedroom door, glancing uncertainly from it to the bed and then back again. The last thing she wanted was to be woken up by Guard rapping on the door to find out where she was.

Sighing under her breath, she walked over to the door and opened it.

Guard was seated at the desk in front of the window, his head bent over the papers spread over it. Rosy watched him for a few, brief seconds. It was a very rare experience for her to have the opportunity to study him unobserved. He was a very handsome man, a very charismatic man, she acknowledged with a tiny thud of her heart. A man most women would love to be married to. But she was not one of them, she told herself hastily. When she married . . .

'What's wrong, Rosy?'

The calm question, asked without Guard's lifting his head or looking at her, made it plain that he was not, as she had imagined, oblivious to her presence at all.

'If you're going to tell me that you can't sleep without your favourite teddy bear,' he added grimly, 'then I'm afraid . . .'

Anger darkened Rosy's eyes. She hadn't slept with her teddy bear for years. Well, not until these last few weeks, when she had felt so devastated by the double loss of her grandfather and father.

'I came to tell you that the bathroom's free,' she informed him with awful dignity.

'Would you like a nightcap before you go to bed?'

His question took her by surprise, her eyes widening slightly and her skin flushing as he put down the papers he had been studying and turned towards her.

She would like a drink, Rosy recognised, but she was acutely conscious of the fact that she was in her nightshirt.

'I—I'd better go and get my dressing-gown,' she told him uncomfortably. 'I——'

She tensed as he stood up, the dark eyebrows lifting sardonically as he came towards her.

'That's very considerate of you, Rosy,' he told her sardonically. 'But hardly necessary. I think I have enough control over my manly passions not to succumb to a fit of lust at the sight of you in your nightwear. After all, it's hardly the most seductive of garments, is it? Not exactly bridal...'

'I suppose when *you* go to bed you wear silk pyjamas,' Rosy defended herself wildly, remembering reading a book in which the hero had been thus clad. 'But for your information——'

She stopped abruptly as Guard started laughing. She had rarely seen him laugh before and for some reason the sight and sound of him doing so now caused a hard, sharp pain to pierce the middle of her chest.

'What is it? Why are you laughing?' she demanded suspiciously.

'No, Rosy,' Guard told her, shaking his head, mirth lightening his eyes so that they seemed more amber than their normal formidable eagle-gold, 'I do not wear silk pyjamas. In fact,' he added dulcetly, watching her closely, 'I don't wear anything at all.'

Rosy couldn't help it; she could feel herself blushing, a betraying wave of scarlet colour washing up over her body and engulfing her in humiliating, self-conscious embarrassment... Not just because of what Guard had said, nor even because of his laughter, but because, unbelievably, unwantedly and untenably, she had just had the most appallingly clear mental image of Guard's naked body—a body which, in that brief, illuminatory vision, had been both arrogantly male and erotically aroused...

She swallowed hard, too caught up in her own emotional shock to be aware of the way Guard's amusement had turned to frowning scrutiny of her suddenly over-pale face and harrowed expression.

'Go to bed, Rosy,' she heard Guard telling her abruptly. 'You've been under a lot of strain recently, and a good night's sleep——'

Suddenly it was all too much for Rosy.

'I'm not a child, Guard,' she told him chokingly. 'I'm a woman, an adult, and it's time you recognised that fact and treated me as one.'

Angrily she blinked away the temper-tears blurring her vision, only to hear Guard saying warningly to her, 'Don't tempt me, Rosy. Don't tempt me.'

CHAPTER SIX

'*MADAME*... So Guard has married at last. I cannot say I blame him,' Monsieur Dubois told Rosy with warm appreciation in his eyes as he shook her hand in response to Guard's introductions.

'And so, how long have you been married, my friend?' he asked Guard in his careful English.

'Not very long,' Guard told him. 'Not very long at all.'

'How angry you must be with me, *madame*,' Monsieur Dubois apologised to Rosy. 'But not so angry as Guard, I suspect. But he is the only person I could trust to do this all-important work for us. It is vital that when we present our case to the authorities we have all the information at our fingertips. These days one doesn't just need knowledge and eloquence, one must have facts, figures, graphs. One must be computer literate or risk the consequences.

'Guard has told you something of our work?' he asked Rosy, as he guided them into his large office overlooking the business centre of the city.

'Something,' Rosy agreed, reluctantly admitting to herself that she was rather enjoying herself. It felt good to be using her brain, her linguistic abilities, and it felt even better knowing she had a skill that Guard could not quite match, she acknowledged ruefully.

As Guard had said, Monsieur Dubois's English was very limited and many of the technical terms he used when he started enthusiastically to explain to her the needs of his organisation were unfamiliar even to her, although she was quickly able to interpret their meaning.

While Guard was following their conversation, she could see from his frowns that he was having difficulties. Without really knowing why, she found herself gently stopping Monsieur Dubois and then turning to Guard, quickly explaining to him what was being said, unaware as she did so of the quiet air of authority and self-assurance in her manner and voice or the maturity it gave her.

When Monsieur Dubois eventually glanced at his watch and exclaimed over the length of time he had kept them, Rosy was surprised to discover how quickly the hours had flown and how much she had enjoyed what she was doing, despite the fact that she had always claimed to her father and to Guard that computers and all that went with them were just not her thing and she was more than happy to keep matters that way.

As they got up to go, Monsieur Dubois turned to Guard and told him, 'My wife and I are giving a small family party this evening. Nothing of any great merit, a simple affair to celebrate our elder daughter's attainment of her degree. I should be delighted if you could both join us, but perhaps you have other plans...?'

'None,' Guard responded promptly. 'What time would you like us to arrive?'

As soon as they were alone, Rosy turned to Guard and protested, 'I can't go to a party, Guard. I haven't brought anything suitable with me to wear.'

'So? Brussels is not on another planet,' he told her drily. 'It does have shops, some very good ones too, I believe. Although I must warn you, Rosy, Monsieur Dubois is the rather old-fashioned sort and I suspect that his obviously very high opinion of you would suffer somewhat were you to dress in something you have liberated from disinterment. He would, I suspect, take it rather as an insult if you turned up at his daughter's party wearing something from a charity shop.'

Rosy turned on him angrily.

'I don't need any lectures from you, Guard, on what I should and should not wear,' she snapped. At home in her wardrobe she had two formal 'little black dresses' bought specifically to wear when she went out with her father or grandfather to various social events. *She* might prefer the comfort of her leggings or the sumptuous feel of the velvets and silks she snapped up from sales and markets, but she would not for the world have upset or embarrassed either of them by wearing something she knew would make them feel uncomfortable.

Guard, though, was a very different matter.

However, she had liked Monsieur Dubois and had recognised for herself, without having to be told by Guard, that he was the old-fashioned sort.

'Unfortunately, I have another meeting this afternoon,' Guard told her, glancing at his watch. 'Otherwise I'd come with you.'

'No, thanks,' Rosy told him curtly. The last thing she wanted was to have Guard standing over her in some dress shop telling her what she should buy.

'What about lunch?' Guard asked her.

'I'm not hungry,' Rosy lied. The euphoria and pleasure she had felt earlier had now gone. Guard hadn't just made her angry with his comments about her clothes, he had—— He had what? Offended her? Hurt her? Impossible. Nothing Guard could say could ever do that. He simply didn't have that kind of power over her.

'If you need some money, Rosy...' Guard offered, but Rosy shook her head.

'I can afford to pay for my own clothes, Guard,' she told him fiercely.

'Yes, I know. You know, Rosy, when you eventually find this perfect, wonderful man of yours, I hope you'll try to remember what prehistoric creatures we males still are in many ways.'

'What do you mean?' Rosy asked him suspiciously.

'I mean that, despite the fact that I cannot think of anything more abhorrent than the kind of clinging woman who wraps herself around you with all the stranglehold of a piece of ivy, we men still enjoy the pleasure of feeling that we can spoil and indulge our woman.'

'By rewarding them for good behaviour by buying them something in the same way that you'd throw a dog a biscuit,' Rosy challenged him, her eyes flashing with contempt and anger. 'The man *I* love will treat me as his equal, Guard—in every way. The last thing he'd want would be for me to feel beholden to him for anything. What we give each other will be given freely.' She broke off, frowning as she saw the way Guard was looking at her.

'What is it? What's wrong?' she asked him uncertainly.

She had never seen him looking at her like that before, never seen him watching her with such intense concentration.

'Nothing's wrong,' he denied harshly. 'But one day, Rosy, you're going to have to grow up and to learn the pain that comes with such idealism. I hope for your sake that, when you do, there's someone around to pick up the pieces . . .'

'Just so long as it isn't you,' Rosy muttered defiantly under her breath. Trust Guard to want to have the last word, to want to put her down.

It was almost an hour now since Guard had dropped her off in the shopping quarter of the city, but so far she had seen nothing she wanted to buy, Rosy admitted as she passed in front of a small boutique to study the dress in the window. Of black velvet and silk taffeta, it had a black velvet bodice with a slightly off-the-shoulder neckline and long, tight sleeves; the bodice fitted tightly, snugly over the waist and the taffeta skirt flared out from just above the hips.

The expensive fabric and the colour gave the dress sophistication, but the skirt made it a younger woman's dress, not the kind of thing which could be worn by Madame la Comtesse, for instance.

Determinedly, Rosy walked into the shop.

'It's a very small size, a couture model,' the saleswoman began doubtfully when Rosy enquired

about the dress. But once Rosy had removed her
coat, she added more warmly, 'But, yes, it will
probably fit you.'

It did . . . just . . . She had had to remove her bra
to try it on, otherwise the straps of her underwear
would have shown, but the bodice of the dress was
stitched in such a way that it gave her just as much
shape as though she had been wearing a bra, Rosy
admitted as she studied her reflection in the mirror.

The richness of the velvet seemed to emphasise
the creamy texture of her skin, the way her curls
caressed the unfamiliar bareness of her exposed
shoulders giving her a slightly vulnerable look that
made her frown slightly.

'It might have been made for you,' the saleswoman enthused.

'It's very expensive.' Rosy hesitated—and she
would have to buy new evening shoes to go with it.
In the end it was the memory of Guard's contemptuous dismissal of her clothes and her taste
that made up her mind for her.

'You won't regret buying it,' the saleswoman assured her, as she packed the dress for her. 'A dress
such as this is an investment, a classic. It will never
date.'

No, but I shall, Rosy reflected wryly as she made
her way back to a shoe shop she had passed earlier.

'You managed to find something, then?' was
Guard's only comment when he picked Rosy up
later at their appointed meeting place.

In addition to the dress, she had several other
packages: shoes, a small evening bag to go with
them, a soft cashmere wrap to wear over the dress
and a pretty seventeenth-century enamelled box she

had noticed in the window of an antiques shop and which she had bought as a small gift for Monsieur Dubois's daughter.

Something more anonymous and safer might have been a wiser choice, she acknowledged as Guard drove out of the city, but the box had been so pretty.

'Damn,' Guard cursed softly, suddenly causing Rosy to glance questioningly at him. 'I meant to ask you to buy something for Gerard's daughter. It's too late to turn back now and——'

'I've got her something,' Rosy told him, turning in her seat to retrieve the parcels she had put on the back seat of the car.

She unwrapped the small box, carefully balancing it on the palm of her hand to show him.

When he said nothing, her heart sank slightly. Obviously he didn't approve. Well, that was just too bad, she decided crossly. She liked it and——

'You know, Rosy, there are still times when you can surprise me. You affect to be uninterested in tradition, you state that you think it's almost a crime for somewhere like Queen's Meadow still to be a private home, and then you go and buy something like this . . .'

'If you don't like it——' Rosy began challengingly, but Guard was already shaking his head in denial of her statement.

'I think it's perfect,' he told her simply. 'Perfect.'

His compliment was so unexpected that Rosy had no idea what to say. She raised her eyes to his and then tensed slightly as she saw the way he was looking at her. It was as if . . . as if . . . A funny, unfamiliar, achey sensation filled her chest, radiating out from just where her heart was.

'Rosy...'

Why, when she had, after all, heard him say her name so many times before, was the sound of his voice suddenly making tiny quicksilver shivers dart up her spine? Why did the sound of it suddenly remind her of a tiger's purr, of soft velvet on smooth skin, of the seductive whisper of a man to his lover...?

Hurriedly, she rushed into speech, desperately pushing away such dangerously contentious thoughts.

'I even managed to remember to buy wrapping-paper, Guard, and a card. Do you know her name? I should have asked Monsieur Dubois. I hope she doesn't think that we're intruding. After all, it is her party and she doesn't know us.'

'Her name, I believe, is Héloise,' Guard responded, his voice suddenly oddly flat. 'As to whether or not she'll resent our presence, I should imagine that is extremely unlikely.'

He didn't speak again until they were driving into the château, and then it was only to remark that, since they had both missed lunch, she must be hungry and he would ask Madame if it was possible for them to have a light meal in their suite.

'Ah, good, you're ready. We should be all right for time, but——'

Rosy tensed as Guard suddenly fell silent as he caught sight of her. She watched him uncertainly from the open bedroom door.

In the shop she had been so confident that the dress was the right choice, but now suddenly she wasn't so sure.

Guard's silence, the way he was looking at her... She swallowed nervously.

'What's wrong? If it isn't suitable...'

'No...' Guard was shaking his head as he turned away from her to pick up the jacket he had placed on the back of a chair and put it on. 'It's fine...'

His voice sounded oddly strained, almost slightly hoarse, Rosy recognised, her attention distracted from her own appearance as she watched the way the movement of Guard's body stretched the white fabric of his shirt against the long, sinewy muscles of his back.

She could see the movement of them beneath his skin through his shirt. Her mouth had gone slightly dry.

She felt breathless and slightly on edge, her senses abruptly and unfamiliarly heightened so that, across the space that separated them, she was suddenly sharply aware of the clean male scent of Guard's body. She gave a small shudder, her pulse suddenly racing, the bodice of her dress tightening slightly against her breasts as though—— She glanced down at her body and gave a small, stifled gasp as she saw the raised outline of her nipples pushing against the velvet fabric, embarrassment flushing her skin as she turned round quickly and hurried back into the bedroom, calling out quickly to Guard, 'My wrap...I almost forgot... It's quite chilly and——'

Could Guard hear the agonised, embarrassed confusion in her voice as clearly as she could? She was not cold at all, but what other explanation could there be for that quite unmistakable physical reaction?

'You're cold?'

Guard was frowning as he followed her into the bedroom.

'I—I was. I'm all right now,' Rosy fibbed as she hugged the wrap protectively around her body. 'I—I thought you wanted to leave,' she reminded him. 'We don't want to be late.'

'Nor do we want to be too early,' Guard told her drily, and then reminded her, 'We are, after all, very newly married...'

When she continued to look blankly at him, he explained grimly. 'Use your intelligence, Rosy. We're newly married and supposedly very much in love. Do you really imagine if that was actually true that there's any way I'd be letting you walk out of here so easily, or that you'd want me to?

'Oh, no——' His voice had dropped to a soft whisper that was almost a hypnotic caress, Rosy acknowledged, as she felt another feverish shudder run through her.

'If we were really what we're supposed to be, right now that stunningly fetching little number you're wearing would be lying on the bedroom floor and you, my dear, would be lying in my arms.'

'Stop it, Guard, stop it,' Rosy protested shakily. 'We're not in love. We're not... It isn't like that...and...'

'No, it certainly isn't,' Guard agreed drily. 'Are you sure you need that wrap?' he added as he walked to the door and opened it for her. 'You look quite flushed...'

Rosy glared at him as she swept past him. He knew quite well what had caused her skin to colour up like that, damn him.

Did he also know that all she had on under her dress was a tiny pair of briefs and a pair of silky, hold-up stockings?

Of course not, how could he? And yet there had been something about the way he had looked at her when he made that comment about the dress lying on the floor and her lying in his arms which, for some reason, had immediately conjured up in her imagination an image of herself almost completely naked, her breasts pressed flat against his chest, while he ran his hands up over her back and told her what he wanted to do to her and what he wanted her to do to him, how he wanted to touch her and how he wanted her to touch him.

As she hurried downstairs another shudder racked Rosy's body, a sharper one this time, saw-edged and painful, making her bite down sharply on her bottom lip in suppression of it.

Her fears that she might feel awkward and uncomfortable among people that she did not know, or that Monsieur Dubois's daughter might resent her father's having invited them, were very quickly dispelled—not only by Monsieur Dubois's and his wife's warm welcome of them, but additionally by the enthusiastic reception they received from Héloïse herself, and Rosy was very quickly drawn into the circle of younger people surrounding her while Guard remained talking with their host and hostess.

Héloise and her friends were a lively, intelligent crowd, very vocal in expressing their ideals and beliefs, teasing Rosy a little—but not unkindly—over what they saw as her nation's reluctance to accept the concept of European citizenship. But Rosy soon discovered that, like her, they too were very concerned about the plight of those less fortunate than themselves, and she was soon absorbed in a discussion with one of Héloise's male friends about the growing problem of the city's homeless.

Renauld, although physically nothing like Ralph—he was much more sturdily built, with thick, curling brown hair and hazel eyes that, Rosy couldn't help but notice, warmed with very open male appreciation when he looked at her—shared very many of Ralph's ideals, leavened with a sense of humour that Ralph tended to lack.

'It seems to me that this is a problem that is common to all nations,' Renauld enthused, as he detached Rosy from the others so that he could talk exclusively to her. 'It occurs to me that we would all have much to gain from exchanging our experiences—sharing what we have learned with one another.'

'Hold a conference, you mean?' Rosy teased him.

'Perhaps something a little less formal than that. I go to Britain occasionally on business, and I should be very interested in visiting your shelter, if that could be arranged.'

'I'm sure it could,' Rosy responded enthusiastically. 'I know Ralph would be very interested to meet you.'

'You are some way out of London, though, from what you tell me,' Renauld began. 'Is there a hotel...?'

'Oh, there'd be no need for that,' Rosy assured him quickly, impulsively. 'You could stay with us.'

'Now that I shall look forward to,' Renauld told her softly.

'Don't take Renauld too seriously,' Héloise warned her teasingly ten minutes later when she came over to join them. 'He is a terrible flirt...'

'You are being very unfair, Héloise,' Renauld protested, unabashed by her comment. 'I am very good at it.'

The three of them were still laughing when Guard came to join them several minutes later.

'I'm afraid it's time for us to leave,' he told Rosy, explaining to the others, 'We have an early flight to catch in the morning.'

'So soon?' Rosy protested, unable to conceal her surprise when Guard told her drily what time it was.

'No need to ask if you enjoyed yourself,' Guard commented once they were in the car heading back to the château.

There was a note in his voice that Rosy couldn't quite place. Not anger or irritation exactly, but something...

'You and young Renauld Bressée certainly seemed to find plenty to talk about.'

Young Renauld...? Rosy's forehead creased in a small frown. During their conversation, Renauld had told her that he had just passed his twenty-fifth birthday, which might make him younger than

Guard, but it certainly didn't merit that odd note of dismissive contempt in Guard's voice.

'He was telling me about a scheme he's involved with that's similar to our shelter,' Rosy responded defensively. 'He seemed very interested in the work we're doing. I—I invited him to come down and meet Ralph the next time he's in London on business,' Rosy added, rushing through the sentence and avoiding looking at Guard as she spoke.

Although why she should feel she had somehow done something wrong—that she had somehow angered Guard—she really had no idea, she told herself firmly.

'And that would be the sole purpose of his visit, would it?' Guard challenged her. 'To meet Ralph?'

Rosy was glad of the darkness of the interior of the car as she felt herself starting to blush slightly.

There was an edge to Guard's voice which underlined her earlier discomfort.

'Of course. Why else would he come?' she demanded.

'Oh, come on, Rosy, even *you* aren't *that* naïve,' Guard told her bitingly. 'It was pretty obvious that Bressée was far more interested in inspecting your bed than those at the shelter.'

'That's not true,' Rosy protested. 'And even if it were——'

She stopped abruptly, suddenly realising that the claim she had been about to make that it was no business of Guard's was no longer wholly true. She had, she recognised, almost forgotten their new relationship.

'Even if it were what?' Guard demanded in a hard voice. 'You aren't interested in him? That wasn't the impression I was getting.'

'We were *talking*, that was all,' Rosy objected. What was wrong with Guard? It was almost as though... As though what? As though he was jealous? Impossible. But even though Rosy assured herself that she had done nothing to merit Guard's attitude towards her, she could already feel the happiness she had experienced at the party starting to drain away. She turned away from Guard and looked bleakly out of the window into the darkness.

She gave a small shiver, remembering what Peter had told her when she had asked him how she and Guard would end their 'marriage'.

'You will have to stay together at least a year,' Peter had warned her. 'Anything less than that and it would be bound to cause suspicion. Initially, you could publicly opt for a "trial separation" and then slowly move from that towards divorce.'

At least a year. Suddenly it seemed a very, very long time.

'There's no point in sulking, Rosy,' she heard Guard telling her tersely. 'You knew what the situation was going to be; the part you'd agreed—chosen, in fact—to play. You're a very new bride, and very new brides do not ignore their husbands and flirt with another man.'

'If you mean Renauld, I was *not* flirting with him,' Rosy protested angrily. 'We were simply talking.' She paused, her eyes flashing as she turned to look at him. He was concentrating on his driving, his gaze fixed firmly ahead of him, his jaw warningly taut.

'*You* may not be able to have a conversation with a woman without flirting with her, Guard,' she told him recklessly, ignoring the message her senses were relaying to her, 'but not *all* men are like you. Thank God,' she muttered under her breath.

'No, they're not,' Guard agreed harshly. 'I doubt your precious Ralph, for instance, or Renauld Bressée, would be prepared to put their reputation at risk in a fraudulent marriage just because——'

'Just because what?' Rosy pressed, when Guard stopped speaking. 'Because I asked you? You're not being fair, Guard. We both know exactly why you agreed to this marriage. You married me because you want Queen's Meadow.'

As she said the words, Rosy felt her throat starting to close up as a wave of intense desolation swept over her.

She hadn't wanted any of this—a fictitious marriage, a husband who didn't even particularly like her, never mind love her. The last thing she had ever wanted was to live a life filled with lies and deceit, to live with a man who felt nothing but irritated contempt for her, who constantly criticised her.

Everything she was having to do went so totally against her deepest principles that it was no wonder she was feeling so uncomfortable with herself, so on edge and miserable.

She had been a fool ever to listen to Peter, to think that——

'And of course the Ralphs and the Renaulds of this world are far too perfect, far too high-minded even to consider doing such a thing, is that what you think?' Guard demanded tautly. 'Don't kid yourself, Rosy,' he warned her. 'If you'd dangled the deeds of Queen's Meadow in front of Ralph for bait, he wouldn't even have thought twice about the moral implications of such a marriage.

'And as for Renauld, did he think to tell you, I wonder, while he was flirting so assiduously with you, that both his and Héloise's family have assumed for years that the two of them will eventually marry? They're distant cousins with complex property and business connections—a marriage between them would tie things up very nicely as far as the families are concerned. Not that that would have stopped him bedding you, of course.'

'Stop it...stop it...' Rosy protested shakily, lifting her hands to cover her ears as she turned her face towards him.

'Why do you always have to be so critical, so cynical?' she demanded passionately. 'Why do you always have to spoil everything for me? I'm not a complete fool, Guard, whatever you might think. Just because I choose—because I *prefer*—to see the best in people, that doesn't mean that I'm not aware.'

As she blinked back the angry tears threatening to flood her eyes she turned away from him, her voice low and slightly rough with pain as she told him, 'All right, so maybe Ralph would have agreed to marry me if I'd offered him Queen's Meadow, but at least *he* wouldn't have wanted the house for himself. He would——'

'He would have destroyed it just as surely as Edward,' Guard interrupted her flatly. 'Grow up, Rosy. Do you honestly, truly believe that Ralph would have cared a single jot for the house or its

history? That he wouldn't have quite happily torn
out the panelling and boarded up the staircase if
that was what it would have taken to get the place
passed as an institution?

'Do you know what would have happened to
Queen's Meadow in those circumstances?' Guard
demanded harshly. 'It would have had to comply
with fire regulations, with safety regulations and
with God alone knows what else as well. And if
you think that *anything*—anything at all—of the
original house would have been recognisable to your
father or grandfather by the time Ralph and his
cohorts had finished with it, then you're a fool.'

'You've never liked Ralph, have you?' Rosy ac-
cused furiously. 'You've always made fun of him,
sneered at him. Well, don't think I don't know why,
Guard——' Rosy stopped abruptly as she half
turned towards Guard to see how he was receiving
her furious tirade.

He didn't look as she had expected—neither
furiously angry nor mockingly contemptuous.

His jaw was clenched as though he was holding
himself under immense control and, as she watched
him, Rosy saw a small muscle jerk slightly, pulsing
against his skin, and the look in his eyes when he
turned his head...

An involuntary shudder seized her as Rosy heard
him invite her softly, 'Go on, Rosy...'

Oh, how she wished she'd never started this conversation, but it was too late to back down now...
Much too late.

'You resent the fact that he isn't like you, that
he doesn't care about money or material things,'
Rosy challenged him bravely. 'Because he's——'

She tensed as Guard started to laugh, so confused by his unexpected reaction that it actually alarmed and upset her more than if he had actually raged furiously at her in denial of her assertion.

'Ralph, not care about money? Then how come he's constantly bombarding *me* with requests for donations for his precious shelter?' Guard taunted her.

'That's different,' Rosy objected. 'He doesn't want it for *himself*. He——'

'No? Is that what you really think, Rosy? All right, I agree he doesn't want money to spend on himself, on *possessions* for himself, but he certainly wants the glory he knows damn well he can get by lifting that pathetically amateur outfit of his into something much more high-profile and professional.'

Rosy bit her bottom lip and looked away from him. Cruel though Guard's comments were, they held a certain hard, gritty core of truth which she herself was far too honest to be able to deny.

To her relief, she realised that they had reached the entrance to the chateau. With any luck, Madame would be lurking in the hallway awaiting their return—or rather Guard's return.

'What—nothing to say for yourself, no passionate defence of your precious Ralph? And why is that, I wonder?' Guard observed cynically as he brought the car to a smooth halt in front of the château.

Rosy did not deign to answer him. What, after all, was the point?

* * *

Tiredly, Rosy reached for the zip of her dress.
Madame had not, after all, been waiting for them
but, once they had reached their suite, Guard had
announced that he had some work to catch up on,
and had promptly seated himself at the desk, totally
ignoring her.

Which, of course, was exactly what she wanted.
So quite why it should have made her feel so bad-
tempered and irritable, she had no idea. It couldn't
be because she had lost an argument to him, nor
even because she was beginning to feel so op-
pressed by the burden of her unfamiliar and unwanted role.

She frowned as the zip on her dress ran smoothly
for a couple of inches and then jammed. Irritably,
she tried to work it free.

Ten minutes later, with her arms aching and the
zip still well and truly jammed, she admitted defeat,
acknowledging that she now had only two options
open to her: either she would have to go to bed in
the dress, or she would have to ask Guard for help.

Reluctantly, she walked towards the bedroom
door and opened it, standing uncertainly just inside
the doorway whilst she studied Guard's downbent
head.

He was seated with his back towards her, making
notes on whatever it was he was reading, his concentration so intense that Rosy hesitated to interrupt him.

Perhaps if she tried the zip one more time...

'Yes, Rosy, what is it?'

Rosy's startled gaze flew to meet Guard's as he
put down his pen and turned towards her.

'It's the zip on my dress,' she told him awkwardly. 'It's stuck and...'

'You'd better come over here and stand in the light where I can see what I'm doing properly,' Guard informed her, motioning her to the centre of the room as he correctly anticipated her request. 'Perhaps you are growing up after all,' he added wryly, as he took hold of her shoulders and turned her round so that he could examine the back of her dress.

'What do you mean?' Rosy demanded stiffly, sensing a fresh taunt and trying to turn round, but Guard was holding her shoulders too firmly for her to move.

It was an odd sensation to feel his fingertips on her bare skin, to see in the mirror over the fireplace the pair of them standing together in a pose which could almost have been one of intimacy... of lovers...

A tiny *frisson* of sensation ran over her skin, an odd and unfamiliar awareness of Guard, not as she always thought of him, but as a man. If it had been Guard whom she had met at the party tonight, for instance, Guard who had flattered her, flirted with her...

Mortified by the extraordinary direction of her own thoughts, she looked down at the floor.

'When did it happen, Rosy?' Guard asked her softly. 'When did preserving a dress become more important to you than preserving your hostility towards me?'

'I don't know what you mean,' Rosy fibbed. Was that a sign of maturity, to decide it was preferable to ask Guard to help rather than tear her dress?

If so, she was beginning to wish that she had made a more immature decision, she acknowledged; she could feel the tension crawling along her spine as she felt the warmth of Guard's breath on the skin of the nape of her neck, as he pushed the weight of her hair out of the way so that he could investigate the jammed zip.

She had read books in which the heroine virtually swooned in ecstasy as the hero pressed impassioned kisses against her nape, but had scornfully dismissed such descriptions as being wildly exaggerated.

Now . . . She swallowed hard, curling her fingers into two small, shocked fists while the warmth of Guard's breath against her skin, as nebulous as mist floating across a meadow, nevertheless had an effect on her senses that was so potent that she——

It was Guard's irritated, 'Keep still, Rosy,' that made her realise what she was doing; she was moving her body back into his as though . . . as though she actually *wanted* . . . as though she was actively seeking to intensify that soft *frisson* of sensual warmth which had bathed her skin in such unexpected sensation.

'Oh, leave it, Guard,' she protested, trying to pull away from him, frantically aware that something had gone wrong, that somehow her body had got its messages all tangled up and that, for some inexplicable reason, it had suddenly decided to react to Guard, to respond to Guard as though——

'Keep still. I can see what the problem is now. There's a small piece of cotton caught in the zip. I think I can work it free, though.'

'Where? Let me see it—I can probably do it myself,' Rosy protested, trying both to pull away from Guard and to swivel round so that she could see over her shoulder but, as she moved forward, Guard managed to free the zip, leaving the soft, supple velvet to slither free of her shoulders and her upper body.

Frantically, Rosy grabbed hold of the velvet, her face flushing as deep a pink as the exposed peaks of her nipples as she stood in mesmerised shock while Guard made a slow and very thorough visual inspection of her half-exposed body.

'Stop it, Guard. Stop looking at me like that,' she blurted out huskily, her voice trembling as much as her body. She wanted to turn and run but for some reason she couldn't move. She could only stand there while Guard's gaze slid lingeringly over her body.

'Like what?' he asked her softly. 'I am, after all, your husband, Rosy, and in reality...'

As he took a step towards her Rosy stared at him with huge, shocked eyes, her nakedness—the original reason for the feeling of excited, nervous sensation crawling slowly through her stomach—forgotten as she felt herself trembling in the golden heat of Guard's gaze, unable to look away from him.

'In reality,' he continued softly, 'have you any idea what it would be doing to me right now, seeing you like this, if we really were man and wife? If you'd deliberately wanted to do so, you couldn't have chosen a more sensually provocative pose, do you know that? The injured innocent clutching her clothes to her body, and yet at the same time exposing——'

Rosy shivered as his gaze dropped to her breasts, hot colour scorching her face as she felt her nipples start to ache.

'If I really were your husband, Rosy, I wouldn't be standing here talking to you,' Guard told her roughly, 'and it wouldn't just be your mouth that would be left swollen and sensitive from my kisses...

'What's wrong?' he taunted her, when he heard the small, shocked gasps she gave. 'Surely you're not so innocent, so naïve, that you didn't *know* that it isn't just the feel of a woman's breasts and nipples in his hands that turns a man on; that the sensation of caressing and suckling a woman's breasts, the sound of her soft cries of pleasure, the——'

'No... No...' Rosy moaned in protest, finally tearing herself free of her imprisonment and turning round to run almost headlong into her bedroom, slamming the door closed behind her and leaning on it while her body shook as though she had a fever and her heart pounded so hard that it made her feel sick.

The hot tears of anguish that crawled silently down her flushed face from behind her closed eyelids had nothing to do with outrage or embarrassment, or anger against Guard for what he had done.

Just for a moment, while she had listened to the hypnotic softness of his voice, she had actually seen his dark head bent over *her* body, his mouth caressing *her*——

Her stifled denial left her throat raw and aching. Shock, bewilderment, guilt, fear—all of them formed a lump of incomprehensible pain and panic that hurt physically as well as emotionally. She had not just mentally visualised Guard's dark head bent over her body, she had also felt...

Trembling from head to foot, her face white with shock, Rosy slowly levered herself away from the door.

What was happening to her? What had happened to her?

She showered quickly.

She walked slowly from the bathroom and got ready for bed, refusing to meet her own reflection in the mirror, conscious of the way the fabric of her nightshirt seemed to rub against the suddenly sensitive peaks of her nipples.

Her face burned with renewed colour.

There was something wrong with her, there had to be, imagining Guard caressing her like that... Imagining herself wanting him to, her body aching for him... needing him...

It was just a trick of her imagination, she assured herself; tomorrow she would feel differently, be back to her normal self...

CHAPTER SEVEN

'WHAT'S wrong, Rosy? Not still sulking because I broke up your flirtation with Bressée, are you?' Guard asked drily.

Cautiously, Rosy turned her head to look at him, reaching for her seatbelt as she did so, when the stewardess announced that they would shortly be landing.

Had Guard really forgotten what had happened last night? The way he'd looked at her, the things he had *said* to her?

He was frowning slightly as he fastened his own seatbelt, a hint of impatience tightening his mouth.

It seemed almost impossible this morning to believe that he was actually the same man who had made her so shockingly, so sensuously—aware of him, and of herself, of her sexuality, her vulnerability.

Had she perhaps overreacted to the whole incident, built it up in her own shock and embarrassment into something much more than it had actually been? Had she been lying awake half the night, dreading having to face Guard in the morning, dreading what he might say, unnecessarily?

It had almost been something of a let-down when he had made no reference at all to the incident, calmly behaving towards her just as he had always behaved, treating her more like an irritating child than a——

Than a what? A woman? A nervous skein of hair-fine sensations tightened ominously in her stomach, her face and body suddenly uncomfortably hot.

'Come on, Rosy,' Guard instructed her as the plane bumped down on to the tarmac. 'The last thing we need now is to arrive back looking as though we aren't speaking.'

'I'm *not* sulking,' Rosy told him stiltedly. 'I'm just . . . tired, that's all.'

'Tired—after a two-day business trip? That will raise a few eyebrows,' Guard derided tauntingly, ignoring her self-conscious flush to continue, 'Once we've picked up the car, I'll drop you off at Queen's Meadow, and then I want to go on to my office to go through a few things, and to the apartment. Did you sort out a room with Mrs Frinton?'

Rosy shook her head. She was behaving a bit like an ostrich, she knew, but so far she had not been able to bring herself to deal with the practicalities thrown up by their marriage.

On the night of their wedding she had slept in the room she had occupied since childhood, while Guard had slept in one of the guest-rooms, but she knew that there was no way they could continue to preserve the fiction that their marriage was a love match if they continued to sleep in separate rooms with almost half a mile of corridor between them.

'I—I thought—— There are two guest-rooms with an interconnecting door and, if I made up the beds myself, then Mrs Frinton won't——'

'Mrs Frinton won't what?' Guard interrupted her. 'Mrs Frinton won't guess that we're sleeping in separate beds? That's fine, Rosy, just as long as she doesn't. If it ever gets out that you and I *are* sleeping separately, you can depend upon it that Edward will have his lawyers on to us so fast...'

Rosy shivered.

'Aren't there any rooms with twin beds?' Guard asked her.

'Only in the attic bedrooms,' Rosy told him, 'and it would look odd if we slept up there.'

'Indeed,' Guard drawled.

'Cheer up,' Guard mocked her later, once they were on their way home. 'Remember, it's only for a year and—who knows?—you might even get to like it.'

'Never,' Rosy told him vehemently, and then immediately flushed a bright and betraying red as she remembered how last night, just for a second, she had experienced that dismaying and extraordinary flood of physical desire.

'Be careful, Rosy,' Guard warned her, adding obliquely, 'Some men might be tempted to take that as a challenge, to prove to you that——'

As Rosy stiffened automatically in rejection of his taunt, Guard turned into the drive, breaking off to ask her, 'Isn't that Edward's car?'

'Yes,' Rosy agreed flatly.

'Mm... I wonder what *he's* doing here. Staging a welcome-home party, do you think? How very thoughtful of him.'

'Edward never does anything thoughtful,' Rosy told him grimly. 'He always has an ulterior motive.'

'Mmm... Well, there are no prizes for guessing what it is this time, are there?'

When Rosy looked questioningly at him, Guard explained.

'The house, Rosy, the house.'

'But it's too late for that. He *knows* we're married.'

What was Edward doing at Queen's Meadow? she wondered, worried, as Guard opened the car door for her and she got out. He knew how much she disliked him, how unwelcome his presence would be.

'Smile, Rosy,' Guard reminded her as he opened the heavy front door. 'Smile.'

As he held the door open for her she had to walk so close to him that it looked almost as though his arm was actually draped possessively across her shoulders and, as she turned towards him to tell him that the last thing she felt like doing was smiling, he looked down at her and murmured dulcetly, 'That's better. Now, if you move a bit closer towards me and open your mouth a little, who knows? It *might* almost appear to an onlooker that you're waiting for me to kiss you.'

To kiss her!

Indignation flashed in Rosy's eyes but, before she could say anything, Mrs Frinton came hurrying into the hallway, looking very upset and anxious.

'Oh, Rosy...I mean Mrs...'

'Rosy is still fine, Mrs Frinton,' Rosy assured the older woman. 'You look upset. Is something wrong?'

Before Mrs Frinton could answer, Rosy heard someone coming downstairs. As she look upwards, she realised that it was Edward, smiling his fake, crocodile smile at them.

'Ah, Rosy—and Guard!' he exclaimed, his smile disappearing as he shook his head and told them dolorously, 'Bad news, I'm afraid. We discovered last week that the subsidence at home which we thought was only a minor problem is far, far more serious. In fact, we've had no option but to move out of the house while the surveyors and lawyers get to work sorting everything out.

'Margaret was worried about our moving in here without being able to let you know, but I told her she was being silly. After all, what else are families for if not to help one another out in an emergency? Where else *could* we go? With all my confidential papers and the work I do at home, it would be impossible for us to move into some hotel. The noise alone would play havoc with Margaret's migraines, and then when the boys come home for half-term... No—I said immediately that we should come here.

'Margaret is still at home, supervising the last of the packing, but she should be here soon. I've taken the liberty of instructing Mrs Frinton to prepare Grandfather's suite for us, although of course we'll have to have a couple of beds brought down from the attic floor. We prefer them these days, you know. Margaret doesn't sleep well and...'

Dumbstruck, Rosy stared at him, hardly able to believe what she was hearing.

'Of course I know that you two young people are only just newly married, but I promise you you'll hardly know we're here and you'll find Margaret a big help, Rosy, my dear. She's used to running a large household—organising dinner parties, that kind of thing.'

Rosy drew in a shaky breath, opened her mouth and then closed it again, not trusting herself to speak. Instead, she gave Guard an imploring look. Thank goodness he was here with her. He would know how to deal with Edward, how to make him leave.

But, to her shock, instead of instantly demanding that Edward *did* leave, Guard said almost conversationally to him, 'Rosy's grandfather's suite—that would be the master suite, I take it?'

'Yes, that's right,' Edward agreed affably, and then added with what, to Rosy, was sickeningly fake concern, 'Oh, I did check with Mrs Frinton that you and Rosy weren't using it, of course. She didn't actually seem to know where you'd be sleeping . . .'

A look Rosy didn't like flickered in the sharp, foxy eyes as he glanced from Guard to her and then back to Guard again.

'Of course, the bathroom attached to the master suite leaves a lot to be desired and——'

'Which is why, I'm afraid, you'll have to pick another room,' Guard interrupted him calmly, whilst Rosy's eyes widened in disbelieving shock. What was Guard saying? Why hadn't he told Edward that he couldn't stay—that he must leave!

She tensed as Guard reached out and placed his arm around her, drawing her closer, her body stiffening in outraged rejection as she glowered at him.

'Rosy and I were just discussing our plans for renovating that part of the house on the flight home,' Guard continued. 'In fact I intend to get in touch with the architect tomorrow. To be honest with you, Edward, I should have thought you'd have found the upper storey bedrooms more ap-

propriate. Especially, as you say, with half-term
coming up. And, of course, as you remarked
yourself, Rosy and I are still rather protective of
our privacy... as newly-weds...'

As he spoke, he turned towards Rosy and added
tenderly, 'Isn't that so, my love?'

Fortunately, he didn't wait for her to make any
reply and neither did Edward.

'By the upper storey, I take it you are referring
to the attic bedrooms,' Edward demanded warily,
'the servants' quarters...'

'That's right,' Guard agreed evenly. 'And now
if you'll excuse us, Edward, we have one or two
things we need to attend to. Since you aren't here
as a guest, I know you won't expect us to stand on
ceremony with you. Oh, and I'm afraid you won't
be able to call on Mrs Frinton for any assistance.
I'm afraid I've behaved in what Rosy insists is a
rather chauvinistic fashion and left it to them to
organise the removal of my own possessions from
my apartment and find new homes for them here.
Which reminds me, Edward... I know you won't
take offence but, since we are to be sharing the same
roof, I know you'll understand if I say that the library and study will both be off-limits to you and
your family. As a newly married man, I shall want
to spend as much time as I can with my wife, which
means that I shall be working, as far as possible,
from home.

'You don't have to worry about anything on that
side of things, darling,' Guard added, smiling lovingly down into Rosy's indignant eyes. 'I'll make
all the arrangements with the technicians and so

forth about installing the telex and the computer stuff.

'Mrs Frinton—Rosy and I have both had a tiring few days. Do you think it would be possible for us to have a little light lunch in the winter parlour? I won't ask you to join us, Edward,' Guard continued smoothly. 'I appreciate how busy you must be... Bad luck—about the subsidence, I mean,' Guard added, as Edward watched him warily.

It was only the almost painful pressure of Guard's fingers round her arm that prevented Rosy from exploding into angry speech before they reached the sanctuary of the small, panelled winter parlour, but once they were there and the door was safely closed behind them, she pulled herself out of Guard's restraining hold and demanded tearfully, 'Why didn't you tell Edward to leave? Why did you let him think it was all right for him to stay here? He *can't* stay here, you know that. I don't *want* him here. I don't believe he really doesn't have anywhere else to go. He's just doing this because... because...'

'Go on,' Guard told her grimly. 'Because what?'

'Because he wants to spy on us,' Rosy flashed fiercely. 'Because...'

'Because he's obviously suspicious?' Guard suggested grimly.

Woodenly, Rosy looked away from him.

She was only just beginning to realise the import of Edward's presence at Queen's Meadow and what it really meant. At first she had simply assumed that he had moved in to annoy them, out of spite and malice, but now Guard was making her acknowledge that he could have a far more sinister and dangerous purpose.

As the seriousness of what Guard was saying sank in the colour seeped from Rosy's face, leaving it pale and strained.

'You're saying that he suspects that we're not...that we don't...that our marriage...But he's only guessing,' she protested as she paced the floor nervously and then swung round to look pleadingly at Guard, willing him to agree with her.

'At this stage, yes,' Guard acknowledged. 'But don't underestimate him, Rosy. He's a very dangerous man.'

'If you really think that, then why are you letting him stay here?' Rosy demanded. 'You should have told him to leave.'

'And risk making him even more suspicious? No, I couldn't do that. I warned you that something like this might happen, right at the outset, Rosy.'

'No, you didn't,' Rosy denied passionately. 'You never said anything about Edward's moving in with us or——'

'Not specifically,' Guard agreed. 'But I did point out to you the risks we were taking, and I did warn you, as well, that there was no way I was going to allow my reputation—professional or personal—to be jeopardised by this marriage.

'Don't delude yourself, Rosy. It won't just be Queen's Meadow that we stand to lose. If Edward suspects that he might be able to make a case against us——' He paused, shaking his head. 'People have faced prison sentences for less.'

'Prison...' Rosy's face went white with shock. 'No,' she whispered. 'No... You're just trying to frighten me.'

She tensed and Guard frowned warningly at her as someone knocked on the parlour door.

When Guard opened it to admit Mrs Frinton carrying a large tray, she relaxed slightly, but her tension soon returned when the housekeeper looked uncomfortably at them both and then burst out, 'I don't want to say anything out of place, only I did work for your grandfather for a long time, and it was obvious that he and Mr Edward—— Well, it's just that Mr Edward has been asking an awful lot of questions.'

'What kinds of questions, Mrs Frinton?' Guard asked her calmly.

How could he be so calm after what he had just said to her, the fright he had just given her? she wondered miserably.

Prison. It was impossible. Wasn't it?

'Well, he wanted to know what room you and Rosy would be using, for instance,' she replied. 'He said it was because he didn't want to upset anyone by taking the room you wanted, and he said that he'd noticed how Miss Rosy's things were still in her old room...'

Rosy gasped in outrage. How dared Edward go into her room? If her grandfather were still alive, he would never——

If her grandfather were still alive, none of this would ever have happened. She would have had no need to marry Guard. She would have had no need to lie and deceive.

She could feel the hot, anguished tears burning the backs of her eyes.

'I said as how I didn't know which room you'd be using, but he kept going on about it. Asked which one you'd used after the wedding...' Mrs Frinton flushed uncomfortably as he looked at them both.

'It's all right, Mrs Frinton,' Guard assured her quickly. 'As a matter of fact we were going to discuss with you which room we shall be using. As I'm sure you'll understand, there are certain rooms which, for emotional reasons, Rosy doesn't want to use. Her father's bedroom, for instance, and her grandfather's. I've already explained to her that I can hardly share the bed in her present room,' Guard added softly, causing Rosy to give him a flushed and indignant glare. They had discussed no such thing, and if he thought he was being funny... Obviously Mrs Frinton knew they wouldn't be using that room. It only had a single bed in it, for one thing.

'We had thought we'd walk round the house together and make our choice that way, although I suspect whichever room we choose will only be a temporary arrangement, since most of the bathrooms need modernising. I personally rather like large Edwardian baths—for a variety of reasons,' Guard added wickedly, with a look at Rosy that made both her and Mrs Frinton blush, 'but Rosy insists that she would prefer something a little more modern and I must admit that I'm going to miss the high-powered shower in my apartment...'

Rosy waited until Mrs Frinton had gone, angrily shaking her head when Guard asked her if she wanted something to eat, wondering how on earth he could so calmly tuck into the sandwiches Mrs Frinton had made, for all the world as though nothing was wrong.

'You *know* we've already decided which rooms we were going to use,' she burst out.

'*Were* being the operative word,' Guard interrupted her quietly, putting his plate to one side and getting up. 'Things are different now, Rosy, which is why, for the duration of Edward's and his family's stay here, you'll be sleeping in my bedroom.'

'*Your* bedroom?' Rosy questioned uncertainly. 'But where will you sleep?'

She had already guessed the answer, and the look he gave her confirmed her worst suspicions.

'Oh, no,' she protested quickly. 'No... Not that. I'm not sharing a room with you, Guard—sleeping in the same... No... We can't.'

'We don't have any alternative,' Guard informed her grimly. 'It's either sharing a room *and* a bed with me, Rosy, or potentially sharing one in one of Her Majesty's prisons with someone else.'

'No,' Rosy denied. 'No. You're just trying to frighten me.'

'What? Do you really think I'm so desperate for a woman that I need to frighten *you* into sleeping with me? Grow up, Rosy,' Guard told her sardonically. 'It isn't sex that's worrying me right now. It's fraud.'

Rosy chewed worriedly on her bottom lip.

'You really mean it, don't you?' she asked him slowly. 'You really do think that Edward suspects.' She gave a small shiver, her eyes registering her fear.

'We wouldn't really go to prison, would we, Guard? I mean, it isn't as though——'

'As though what? As though we've done anything wrong in conniving together to deprive Edward of his inheritance? I doubt that the courts would take such a lenient view.' He gave her a wintry look. 'Of course, if you prefer to ignore my advice and take the risk of——'

'No,' Rosy denied quickly. She was really beginning to feel afraid now.

'I'm no more happy about the situation than you are,' Guard told her. 'I agreed to marry you, Rosy, not sleep with you and, believe me, if there'd been any way I could have got Edward to leave without adding fuel to the fire of his suspicions, I would have done so.'

Guard didn't want to sleep with her, to share his bed with her? Rosy frowned as she recognised that she was not finding this information quite as reassuring as she ought.

Those odd feelings that floated, haze-like, just beyond her grasp—were they really chagrin, pique and the hurt of rejection? Surely not!

'So...this room would seem to be the most suitable. Unless you'd prefer one of the others?'

Silently, Rosy shook her head.

She and Guard had just spent an hour inspecting the bedrooms.

Rosy had paused briefly outside the door to the two adjoining rooms which she had originally believed they would occupy, but Guard had firmly taken hold of her arm and drawn her away, murmuring grimly to her, 'Think yourself lucky that

I've managed to insist that Edward isn't sleeping on the same floor as us, otherwise I suspect we'd have him in the room next to us eagerly monitoring every sound—or lack of them.'

When he saw the revulsion darken her eyes, Guard had grimaced cynically.

'You find that offensive. Well, I promise you, it's nothing to what could be dragged up in Court...'

Now they were standing in a large, corner room at the opposite end of the house from the rooms she and her father and grandfather had occupied.

Rosy stood in silent contemplation of the huge, four-poster bed.

Perhaps at one time this room, with its large, comfortable bed, its warm panelling, its fireplace, and even its deep window-seat, had represented sanctuary to another woman—had even, perhaps, been somewhere where she had known love and pleasure—but *she* could not see it like that. She bit down hard on her bottom lip, trying to keep her anguish at bay.

She was afraid, she recognised shakily, afraid for almost the first time in her life. Not of Guard, no matter how much she might balk at having to share a room—and a bed—with him. No, what she feared was the danger he had revealed so trenchantly to her.

'We couldn't... we wouldn't really go to prison, would we?' she asked him in a small voice through dry lips.

'What do you want me to tell you, Rosy? A comforting lie to make you feel better? *You're* the one who keeps telling me that you're a woman and not a child,' he reminded her.

'But if Edward believes that we're sleeping together, that we're really married, then you think that he'll stop being suspicious?' she persisted stubbornly.

'It would certainly give him less grounds for his suspicions,' Guard agreed. 'But don't under-estimate Edward, Rosy. He's a liar and a cheat and, like all liars and cheats, he knows very well how to recognise those traits in others.'

'I don't think anyone's slept in this room since Gramps's seventieth birthday party,' Rosy told Guard in a strained voice as she ignored his comment and walked over to the larger of the room's two windows.

The velvet covering the window-seat was old and faded, like the curtains and the bed-hangings, but it still had a richness, a softness, an air of luxury about it that no modern fabric could match.

'This velvet came from Venice,' Rosy told Guard stiltedly. 'My grandmother bought it when she and Gramps were there on their honeymoon...'

'Yes, I know,' Guard responded quietly.

There was a note in his voice that Rosy had never heard before. He sounded almost as though he felt compassion for her... pity...

'Rosy, I know that this isn't easy for you...'

Rosy stiffened as she recognised that he had left the bed and was coming up behind her.

If he touched her now—— Her spine tensed as she turned away from the window, rushing into hurried speech.

'We'll need fresh bedding and...and towels. There are some linen sheets, I think, that should be large enough—Irish ones that were a part of my great-grandmother's trousseau. It's a very big bed...'

'A very big bed,' Guard agreed. 'With more than enough room in it for both of us and a couple of bolsters.'

'Bolsters?'

Puzzled, Rosy turned round.

'Yes, bolsters,' Guard agreed. 'You put them down the middle of the bed to split it into two. At one time, no romantic novel worthy of its name would have been without them, or so I've heard,' Guard told her drolly.

Rosy gave him a wan smile.

'We couldn't use them even if we had any,' she told him. 'Edward might see them...' Her voice cracked suddenly, hot tears flooding her eyes. 'I never dreamed it would be like this,' she cried miserably. 'I just wanted to protect the house, that's all.'

'Yes, I know. Come on, have a good cry. It will make you feel better,' Guard told her, crossing the floor and drawing her into his arms with surprising gentleness.

She had no time to reject him or to protest; this was a Guard she had not previously known, she recognised as she succumbed to the comfort of being held firmly in his arms, of having the warm solidity of his body to lean on.

Being held like this by him brought home to her how alone she now was—her father and her grand-

father both gone, no loving, paternalistic figure for
her to turn to with her troubles any more.

This knowledge made her tears flow faster,
soaking through the fine white cotton of Guard's
shirt.

'It wasn't supposed to be like this,' she protested, half hiccuping the words.

'I know.'

How comforting Guard's voice sounded, as
comforting as the protective way he was holding
her.

'Guard, I'm so afraid. What are we going to do?'

The whispered admission made his arms tighten
slightly around her. Guard must be afraid as well,
Rosy acknowledged, otherwise he would never have
stressed the danger of their situation to her so
strongly.

'Well, there *is* one way we could get Edward off
our backs—permanently.'

Rosy tensed and lifted her head from his
shoulder, staring up at him in shocked disbelief.

'Tell the truth, you mean? Admit that we deliberately set out to deceive him? No . . . We couldn't
do that.'

Rosy shivered as Guard suddenly released her,
stepping back from her and turning his back on
her, his voice familiarly harsh, his whole manner
towards her hurtfully distancing.

'No, you're right, we couldn't,' he told her.
'Look, I've got to go into my office, Rosy,' he said
crisply, glancing at his watch. 'I'll get back just as
soon as I can. With any luck, Edward will be too
busy transporting his confidential papers to hound
you too much while I'm gone.'

What had happened to the closeness, the warmth which had seemed to exist between them only moments ago? Rosy wondered, shivering slightly. Where had it gone?

What she ought to be asking herself was where it had come from in the first place, she told herself tiredly when Guard had gone. And if it had actually existed at all, or if she had simply imagined it.

There was quite definitely no history of any emotional rapport between them—far from it—and yet she could have sworn, when Guard had taken hold of her, that he had genuinely wanted to comfort her, to reassure her, to be close to her.

Guard wanting to be close to her? Now she *was* letting her imagination run away with her.

No doubt in reality he was cursing the day he had ever been foolish enough to agree to marry her.

'I just hope you appreciate what we're doing for you,' she whispered to the house, gently touching the panelling as she opened the bedroom door.

'There's something about a proper bed made up with proper bed-linen,' Mrs Frinton exclaimed in satisfaction as she stepped back to admire both her own and Rosy's handiwork.

The four-poster bed, along with every piece of furniture in the room, including the panelling, had been polished; the windows had been cleaned; the brass taps on the huge Edwardian bath and basin rubbed to a shine and, finally, the bed made up with linen sheets, blankets and a traditional hand-embroidered bedspread.

Because of the bed's width, it had taken both of
them to make it up, and Rosy grimaced inwardly
at Mrs Frinton's comment, remarking that modern
duvets certainly made life a lot easier.

'You'd have a hard time getting a duvet for a bed
this size,' Mrs Frinton responded. 'Big enough for
a whole family, it is.'

A family. A small shadow touched Rosy's eyes
as she glanced down at the bed.

There was a hollow, empty feeling inside her, a
hard, painful sense of being very alone, of not
having anyone close to her for her to share her life
with. It was a feeling she had never experienced
before, a feeling of which, she recognised on a small
frisson of disquiet, she had first become aware this
afternoon, just after Guard had removed the protection of his arms from around her body.

When her grandfather had made his will, he had
wanted the house to stay in the family, to be lived
in, to be loved by his descendants.

Guard would love it and live in it, Rosy told
herself firmly. Guard would protect the house and
eventually his children would grow up here.

Guard's children, but not hers. Hers would only
know of the house through her memory of it.

The intensity of the desolation that swept over
her frightened her all the more because she wasn't
entirely sure what was causing her misery—the
thought of her children not growing up at Queen's
Meadow, as she had done, or the thought that
Guard's children would.

And yet she had never previously felt possessive
about the house, far from it. About the house, or
about Guard?

The small *frisson* became a deep shudder, a small, painful flowering of knowledge unfurling inside her, which she quickly and fearfully tried to smother with a flurry of small-talk to Mrs Frinton.

It was just Edward's presence in the house that was making her so anxious and unhappy, she told herself. That was all.

CHAPTER EIGHT

'WELL, now, I expect you two will want to be left on your own.'

The only smile Edward gave Rosy made her stomach heave with loathing.

'Well, don't hang about, then, Margaret,' he ordered his wife, his pseudo good humour quickly disappearing as he turned away from Rosy and glared across the dinner table at his wife.

'There's still a lot of stuff to be sorted out. How on earth you manage to be so useless I really don't know.'

Rosy tensed with angry resentment on Margaret's behalf as the older woman's thin, sallow face flushed and she immediately and awkwardly stood up, hurrying to obey her husband's demands.

Automatically, Rosy tried to help her, pushing her own chair back and saying quickly to her, 'Why don't you leave it until tomorrow, Margaret? I'm not due to go down to the shelter until the afternoon, so I could give you a hand, and I'm sure Mrs Frinton wouldn't mind helping us out as well——'

'The shelter...' Edward's eyebrows rose as he rudely interrupted Rosy. 'Dear me, I should have thought Guard would have put a stop to your going down there. With all the riff-raff who use the place, there's no knowing what you could——'

134

'They are *not* riff-raff.' Rosy cut him off angrily. 'None of them wanted to be made homeless, Edward; none of them wanted to have to depend on others, on the State for charity and...'

She tensed as Guard reached for her hand, wanting to snatch her fingers out of his grasp but not quite daring to do so. Her work at the shelter had always been a slightly sensitive issue, especially with her grandfather, who had been inclined to be old-fashioned in his views, and Rosy suspected that Guard shared both his and Edward's opinion that what they were trying to achieve with the shelter was a waste of time and money.

Defensively, she tried to pull her hand out of Guard's, unwilling to hear him adding his criticism to Edward's, but instead of supporting Edward as she had anticipated, he said firmly, 'Rosy is quite right, Edward, and these people deserve not just our sympathy but our practical support as well. But quite apart from that, even if I did not share Rosy's belief in what she does, I would hardly have the right to interfere. Rosy is my wife—an equal partner in our relationship. I respect her right to make up her own mind about what she does and does not do. After all, if there isn't mutual respect and trust between a man and a woman, how can there be love?'

Rosy turned round to look at Guard in astonishment. She had never expected to hear him express such views. They were so completely alien to the Guard she thought she knew; the Guard she had always dismissed as domineering and arrogant.

Out of the corner of her eye, she just caught sight of Margaret's face with its wistful, unhappy expression.

Poor Margaret. How tragic to be married to a man like Edward, and how even more tragic if she had actually once loved him.

The small incident stayed in her mind and when she and Guard were eventually on their own she turned impulsively to him and asked him uncertainly, 'Did you mean what you said earlier? About... about believing that... that loving someone means respecting and trusting them?'

The thoughtful look he gave her made Rosy wish she had not raised the issue.

'That's a first for you, isn't it?' Guard asked her drily. 'Actually acknowledging that *I* might have thoughts and feelings instead of...?'

'Instead of what?' Rosy pressed.

He simply shook his head and told her calmly, 'Yes. I do believe that respect and trust go hand in hand with love—with *genuine* love, that is, not the far more common and ephemeral lust that so many people confuse it with.

'Loving someone means loving them as they are, accepting them as themselves, *wanting* them to be themselves instead of trying to change them to fit into our own preconceived image of what the person we love must be. It means loving them *because* of the person they are, not in spite of it...'

He frowned as Rosy gave a small shiver and asked her softly, 'What is it, what's wrong?'

'Nothing,' Rosy lied, knowing that she dared not allow herself to look directly at him just in case he saw the emotion in her eyes and guessed how much his words had affected her.

Would anyone ever love her like that, so completely and so honestly?

It shocked her that it should be Guard of all people who had described love to her in exactly the same terms as she would have chosen herself; Guard who, had she been asked, she would have insisted quite unequivocally could not possibly have understood—never mind shared—such ideals.

'You look tired,' she heard Guard telling her. 'Why don't you go to bed before Edward decides to inflict his company on us? He's probably had enough of bullying Margaret.'

'Do you think she once loved him?' Rosy couldn't resist asking quietly.

'Him? No,' Guard told her decisively, shaking his head. 'The man she might have been deceived into thinking he was? I suspect, unhappily for her, yes. Poor woman...'

'I wonder why she stays with him when he's so horrible to her.'

'He's probably damaged her sense of self-esteem and self-worth to such an extent that she can't leave. And then, of course, there are her sons.'

'He's such a horrible person. He *likes* hurting her, bullying her...'

'Yes,' Guard agreed, adding warningly, 'And that is nothing compared with what he's likely to want to do to us if he ever discovers the truth about our marriage.'

Rosy gave a small shiver.

'Don't, Guard,' she begged, her apprehension showing in her eyes.

'It's all right,' Guard reassured her. 'There's no reason why he should find out, not if we're both . . . careful . . .'

'I never thought he'd do anything like this,' Rosy whispered. 'Move in here and——'

'Stop worrying about it,' Guard told her. 'You're supposed to be a deliriously happy bride, remember?'

Rosy gave him a wan smile.

'I suppose it could be worse,' she agreed, forcing another smile. 'After all, if we were really in love, having Edward or anyone else here would be the last thing we'd want . . .'

'The very last thing,' Guard agreed softly.

For some reason that Rosy couldn't quite define, something in the way he was looking at her and the tone of his voice suddenly made her heart skip a beat and her face flush slightly.

'You're right,' she told him huskily, 'I should go to bed. I *am* tired . . .'

'I'll be an hour or so yet,' Guard responded. 'I've got one or two things I need to do.'

'Good—goodnight then,' Rosy mumbled awkwardly, avoiding looking at him as he held the door open for her.

She was halfway down the upper corridor when she heard Edward calling her name. Immediately she tensed, taking a deep breath before turning round.

'Having an early night?' Edward asked her mockingly as he reached her.

Somehow or other, Rosy managed to stop herself from responding in the way she would have liked, saying quietly instead, 'I thought Margaret looked very tired at dinner tonight, Edward. It must be quite a strain for her, having to move over here at such short notice.'

'Oh, she likes to make a fuss about nothing,' Edward responded dismissively. 'She's like that. Where's Guard?' he asked inquisitively.

'He had one or two things to do downstairs,' Rosy answered.

The way Edward was looking at her made her feel both uncomfortable and angry at the same time.

'Not getting tired of you already, is he?' he taunted. 'You'll have to watch him, you know, Rosy. A man with his reputation...'

'Guard chose to marry *me,*' Rosy responded fiercely. 'Any past relationships he might have had are exactly that, Edward—past.'

She felt rather proud of her response and it certainly seemed to rattle Edward.

'What are you doing here on this floor anyway?' she demanded, seizing her advantage.

'I was just on my way down to collect some of the stuff we unloaded into the garages earlier,' Edward told her. 'I want to get everything inside as soon as I can. It will take me at least a couple of hours yet to move it all. You know, Rosy, you really should have thought a little harder before you rushed into marriage with Guard. You're taking a very big risk, you know.'

Rosy could feel her heart starting to pound anxiously.

'What—what do you mean?' she challenged Edward, hoping that he wouldn't see the nervous guilt in her eyes.

What was she going to do—to say—if he told her
that he knew why she had married Guard? *Why*
had she let him corner her like this when Guard
wasn't here? Why had she...?

'You *know* what I mean,' Edward told her softly.
'Oh, I can understand why you fell for him. Guard
certainly knows how to handle a woman, but then
of course he's had a lot of practice... But have you
asked yourself this, Rosy—*why* has he married
you?'

'Because he loves me,' Rosy replied instantly.

Just for a moment she had thought that Edward
had actually guessed the truth.

But even if he hadn't, it was obvious that he suspected something, Rosy acknowledged as she turned
on her heel and left him.

With only the lamps on in the bedroom, the large
room looked surprisingly intimate and cosy.

It was the bed that did it, Rosy decided. It
looked...

It looked...

Hastily she averted her gaze from it. Well, what
it *didn't* look was as though it had been designed
for one solitary celibate sleeper. Very, very much
the opposite...

Reluctantly, Rosy stepped out of the bath and
reached for a towel. She had felt so luxuriously relaxed lying there, lapped by the soft, warm water,
that she could almost have fallen asleep.

Still smiling, she walked into the bedroom to
collect her nightshirt, and then stopped, her smile
disappearing abruptly as she remembered that her

nightshirt, along with the rest of her clothes—and her underclothes—was still in her old bedroom.

In all the fuss of getting this room ready, the anxiety of Edward's unexpected and unwanted descent on them, she had completely forgotten about moving her things.

She looked uncertainly at the bedroom door, nibbling at her bottom lip. Dared she take the risk of running down the corridor, dressed just as she was with a towel wrapped about herself, to retrieve her clothes, or should she get dressed just in case Edward saw her?

She was still debating the matter when the bedroom door opened and Guard walked in.

Rosy stared at him.

'I thought you said you'd be a couple of hours,' she reminded him, making sure that the towel was completely secure.

'I did, but Edward was sniffing around making pointed comments about bridegrooms and neglected brides.'

'Is he still there?' Rosy asked him anxiously.

'Yes. Apparently he's got some stuff he wants to get upstairs tonight. Why?'

Rosy grimaced uncomfortably.

'I forgot to move my things from my old room.'

Guard gave a small, dismissive shrug.

'So you can move them in the morning. If he says anything, you can just tell him that there wasn't time to move them before the wedding.'

Rosy wriggled uncomfortably within the confines of her towel. 'No,' she contradicted him, 'you don't understand. I—I haven't got anything. *Any-thing*,' she repeated insistently. 'My—my underwear, my nightshirt, they're all still in my old room, and so is the bag I brought back from Brussels,' she added unhappily.

She winced as she saw the look Guard was giving her.

'I just forgot all about it,' she defended herself. 'What with finding Edward here and then having to get this room organised. I'll have to go and get them.'

'No,' Guard told her sharply.

'But I've *got* to have my nightshirt,' Rosy protested, panicking. 'I haven't got anything to sleep in. It's all right for you, you've got your things.'

She and Mrs Frinton had unpacked the bag Guard had brought over from his apartment with some of his clothes in it, even though he had told them both wryly that he didn't expect them to do so.

'A new bride, Rosy,' Guard informed her now, 'does not leave her husband's bed to go in search of a nightshirt, and to do so would be especially unwise in our present situation, with Edward still prowling about. No... I'm afraid that for tonight at least you'll just have to sleep as you are—in your skin.'

Rosy stared at him.

'No,' she choked. 'I can't...'

'Of course you can,' Guard contradicted her. 'I do it all the time.'

Aghast, Rosy glanced from him to the huge bed and then back again.

'I am not sleeping with you in that bed without either of us having... With both of us... Without either of us having any clothes on,' she told him primly.

'Why not?' Guard asked her calmly.

Rosy stared at him in baffled confusion.

What did he mean, why not? Wasn't it obvious?

'Well, because it just isn't done,' she floundered unhappily.

Guard's eyebrows rose.

'Is that so? It seems to me that you have some very odd views on marriage, Rosy. *That*, I can assure you, is *exactly* how it's done.'

He paused, watching her while she curled her toes protestingly into the carpet and the blush she could feel warming her body swept over her from head to toe.

'There is nothing—nothing,' Guard repeated softly, 'which is quite so sensual, so pleasurable as the feel of skin against skin, body against body.'

An odd, dizzying sensation seemed to have infiltrated her body and, along with it, a sort of aching, yearning need spiked with a bitter-sweet, sharp spiral of dangerous excitement. Skin against skin, Guard had said, body against body. He had not been speaking personally at all, so why did she suddenly feel hot all over, her imagination shocking her with mental images of *their* skin, *their* bodies...?

As fresh heat filled her face, Rosy retreated to the far side of the bed.

'What is it, Rosy?' he teased her. 'Afraid your unbridled desire for me might get totally out of control at the thought of my vulnerable, naked body in bed next to you, and that you might...'

Rosy knew that he was only joking, laughing at her, but, for some extraordinary reason, instead of being relieved by his attempt to lighten things, she actually felt——

She swallowed hard, too distressed by her emotions to allow herself to give them a name.

Not trusting herself to speak, she reverted instead to childhood, picking up a pillow from the bed and hurling it angrily at Guard.

He caught it with derisive ease, openly laughing at her.

'Baby,' he taunted her. 'Well, if that's the way you want to behave, Rosy...'

He moved so quickly she had no chance to evade him as he scooped her up off the floor and held her at arm's length, still laughing at her as she kicked out protestingly, demanding to be set free.

Still laughing, Guard started to comply with her request but, as he released her waist, and her toes touched the floor, Rosy felt the towel start to slide from her body.

It was like that moment in the château bedroom all over again, only this time... This time...

As she struggled frantically with numb fingers to resecure the towel, she heard Guard saying quietly, 'Maybe you're right, Rosy. Maybe sleeping together isn't such a good idea after all, but I'm afraid we just don't have any choice,' he added, his voice suddenly unfamiliarly harsh. '*Neither* of us has any choice, so we'll just have to make the best of things. At least the damn bed's big enough to allow us both some degree of privacy...'

No wonder Guard looked so angry with her, Rosy acknowledged, as he disappeared into the bathroom, leaving her to crawl miserably beneath the bedclothes. If she hadn't been such an idiot and forgotten to move her clothes...

Her throat felt tight with suppressed tears and her feet were cold, she decided miserably. Why on earth had she been such an unsophisticated idiot and made all that fuss about not having her nightshirt? It was obvious from the way Guard had acted, the way his manner had changed after he had seen her naked body, that he didn't have the smallest degree of sexual desire for her.

Which, of course, was just as it should be—and just how she wanted it to be, wasn't it...? Of course it was, she told herself firmly as she lay as close as she could to the cold edge of the bed and closed her eyes, trying to ignore the sounds coming from the bathroom.

Unlike her, Guard obviously preferred to shower. She gave a small, unhappy shiver as she was unexpectedly tormented by a mental image of his naked body, his skin gleaming wetly like heavy, rich satin.

She didn't want him. Of course she didn't... She didn't even like him, never mind love...

With a small, defensive sob, Rosy reached for one of the spare pillows and held it down firmly over her ears, blotting out the tormenting sounds from the bathroom.

CHAPTER NINE

Rosy woke up with a start. Someone was knocking on the bedroom door. She tensed as she recognised Edward's voice calling Guard's name and her own.

Guard. Her tension increased as she recognised that the reason she felt so deliciously warm and had no doubt been so reluctant to wake up was that, somehow or other, she had relinquished her hold on the edge of the bed and was now lying virtually in the centre of it, curled up next to Guard.

'It's all right, Rosy, you stay there. I'll go and find out what he wants,' she heard Guard telling her as he sat up and switched on the bedside lamp, swinging his legs on to the floor at the same time. Rosy hastily averted her gaze from his naked body.

A warm glow suffused her skin as she didn't look away quite quickly enough and was left with a vivid image of the awesome perfection of his body.

Out of the corner of her eye, she saw him pick up his robe from the end of the bed and shrug it on, and expelled a small sigh of relief.

'Yes, Edward, what it it?' she heard Guard asking grimly, as he half opened the door, positioning his body, she noticed gratefully, so that Edward couldn't see past him into the room. But Edward, it seemed either couldn't interpret Guard's body language or preferred not to do so, and virtually pushed past him, exclaiming, 'It's Margaret! Is Rosy...?'

He seemed more disappointed than relieved to
see her there, Rosy recognised as Edward came to
an abrupt halt at the foot of the bed.

Uncomfortably conscious of her nudity, Rosy
clutched the bedclothes protectively to her body as
Guard demanded curtly, 'What is it, Edward?
What's wrong with Margaret?'

'Er... she's got a headache, and I was wondering if Rosy had some aspirin or something. We
can't seem to find ours.'

'Headache?' Guard's eyebrows snapped sharply
together in anger. 'You wake us up at two o'clock
in the morning because your wife's got a headache?'

'Well, it's more of a migraine than a headache,'
Edward defended himself.

'If Margaret suffers from migraines, I doubt very
much that mere aspirin would do anything for
them,' Guard told him.

Rosy struggled to sit up slightly, and keep her
body covered up at the same time as she told him
quickly, 'I'm sorry, Edward, but I don't have anything like that up here. You should find some
downstairs in the medicine cupboard in the kitchen.
Poor Margaret,' she added sympathetically. 'She
must be in dreadful pain...'

'Yes, well, I'll go down and see if I can find
something for her,' Edward told them. 'I'm sorry
if I disturbed you...'

He didn't look sorry at all, Rosy reflected uneasily as Guard walked with Edward to the door
and very pointedly opened it for him.

'Poor Margaret,' Rosy repeated nervously as
Guard walked back towards the bed.

'Poor Margaret indeed—if in fact she *does* have a migraine,' Guard responded grimly. 'Personally, I doubt it, and in fact——'

'What do you mean?' Rosy asked him anxiously, her body suddenly tense with apprehension. 'Are you trying to say that Edward woke us up deliberately so that he could check——?'

'That we were actually sleeping together? I think there's a strong possibility,' Guard confirmed grimly.

The severity of Guard's expression made Rosy's heart miss an anxious beat.

Looking away from him, she nibbled worriedly at her bottom lip.

The bed dipped slightly beneath Guard's weight as he got in beside her and switched off the bedside lamp.

'Guard,' Rosy asked him in a small voice, 'how suspicious do you think Edward really is? I mean, he must have guessed something, mustn't he, to come down here...?'

'It looks like it,' Guard agreed after a small pause but, as Rosy made a small distressed sound, he added, 'But there's no point in jumping to conclusions, or in worrying, and after all, nothing he saw in here tonight could possibly have given him the confirmation he was looking for—far from it.'

Rosy knew that Guard was speaking the truth, but she still felt disturbed and on edge.

'Edward's gone now. Go back to sleep,' Guard told her.

'I can't,' Rosy admitted shakily. 'I'm afraid, Guard,' she added. 'What if Edward does find out and...?'

She heard the rustle of the bedclothes as Guard turned over and switched on the lamp.

'There's nothing for you to be afraid of,' he told her quietly as he looked down at her.

He was half sitting up, the bedclothes round his waist, the upper half of his body exposed as he leaned over her.

'What is it, Rosy? You're not crying, are you?' he asked her softly.

Quickly Rosy shook her head, but she knew he must have seen the suspicious shine in her eyes.

'You said we'd go to prison,' she told him in a stifled voice, by way of explanation.

'I said we *could*,' Guard corrected her.

Rosy saw his chest expand as he drew in a deep breath. An odd *frisson* of sensation ran across her skin, as delicate as the velvet touch of a cat's sheathed paw and yet, at the same time, so powerful that she rushed into speech to try to stifle it.

'I never thought I could ever be so afraid of someone like Edward,' she told Guard huskily.

'And I never thought I'd see the day when you admitted that you were afraid of anything—especially to me,' Guard responded. 'It's all right, Rosy. I promise you that everything's going to be all right. Come here...'

When he reached out and took her in his arms, Rosy was too surprised to speak.

How long was it since anyone had held her like this, comforted her like this? she wondered shakily as Guard reached up and smoothed her hair back off her face.

'I still can't believe that Edward would actually do something like that,' she whispered. 'That he would actually come here in the middle of the night to check . . .'

'Stop thinking about it. He's gone now,' Guard soothed her.

'Yes, I know,' Rosy responded, lifting her head from his shoulder to look anxiously into his eyes. 'But, Guard, if we hadn't been sharing the bed . . . If you'd been sleeping in the chair or if I'd been——'

'Wearing your nightshirt,' Guard interrupted her wryly. 'As I said, Rosy, forget it.'

'I can't,' Rosy protested, shivering suddenly and burying her face against Guard's shoulder. 'I can't.'

'Rosy.'

Rosy tensed as she heard the harsh tension in Guard's voice, but she didn't respond to the pressure of his hand on her shoulder urging her away from his body. She didn't *want* to move away from him, she recognised; she didn't want to go back to her own cold and lonely side of the bed. She didn't want . . .

'Rosy.'

Her body quivered as the warm gust of Guard's fiercely expelled breath touched her skin.

'Rosy . . .'

His voice sounded different now—thicker, slower, less determined, more——

Her heartbeat had become dangerously unsteady. The warmth of Guard's breath against her skin told her just how close his mouth was to her throat, so close that if she just moved the tiniest little bit . . .

She shivered in sharp pleasure, her pulse-rate accelerating frantically as she felt Guard's mouth brush her skin.

'Rosy...you know what's going to happen if you don't let go of me, don't you?' she heard Guard warn her softly.

Let go of him? Her eyes widened in shock as she realised what he meant. Somehow, without knowing she had done so, she had curled one hand possessively around the hard muscles of his forearm, or at least as far round them as her slender fingers could stretch. Let go of him? But she didn't *want* to let go of him, she recognised with a shiver of intense sensual awareness. She wanted to stay exactly where she was with his body next to hers, his hands...his mouth...

'Guard.'

Could *he* hear the shocked confusion in her voice, the need...the desire...?

Her eyes widened as his hand slid beneath her hair to cup her face and she saw that he had. His own eyes looked darker, brighter, the pupils enlarged.

Nervously, Rosy caught her bottom lip between her teeth.

'Don't do that,' she heard Guard protest in a thick, slurred voice.

And then it was his mouth, his teeth, that released her tortured lip from its bondage, explored and caressed it, driving her to such an unimagined frenzy of need that Guard had to hold her down against the pillow while he satisfied her frantically whispered pleas to be kissed properly and not so cruelly teased.

'Properly... Like this do you mean, Rosy?' she heard him demanding rawly before his mouth covered hers.

No one had ever kissed her so intensely, so demandingly before, but it was the strength of her own passion that shocked her, not Guard's. It was as though her untutored body had somehow developed a wilful sensuality of its own.

Without any conscious effort on her part her body arched, her arms clung, her lips parted and, if she could have done so, a stunned, shocked part of her recognised, she would have wrapped herself so intimately and erotically around Guard that——

If she *could* have done so? She trembled as Guard dragged his mouth away from hers and muttered roughly, 'My God, Rosy, you witch. If I didn't know better I'd——'

He didn't finish his sentence; the hand which had been caressing the smooth skin of her back had come to rest against the side of her breast and, without even having to think about it, Rosy had moved just enough for the warmth of his palm to cover the hard point of her nipple. The urge to move against that warmth, deliberately create an erotic friction that could only intensify the sharp, deep yearning flooding her body, was so intense that she had to stifle the vocal expression of it in her throat.

But Guard must have heard it, or knew without having to hear it, because his fingers were already caressing her nipple, his mouth moving downwards over her body.

As she felt his mouth carefully take the place of his fingers, drawing her nipple with agonising

slowness into a moist caress, Rosy shivered helplessly, her eyes betraying her sensual vulnerability
when Guard slowly released her nipple and then
told her rawly as he circled the damp areola with
one fingertip, 'That's nothing, Rosy. But this...'

As his mouth recaptured her nipple and he started
to suckle rhythmically, the feeling that poured
through her was so intense that her whole body
twisted frenziedly, her nails digging into Guard's
skin.

In response, Guard's suckling became deeper and
more urgent; he pushed the bedclothes away from
her body, his hand caressing the curve of her hip,
sliding round to press firmly against the lower half
of her stomach, just as though he knew that the
ache he was causing in her breast had its beginning
right there, deep inside her body where his hand
rested, as though he knew that somehow, its
warmth, its pressure did something to ease a little
of the almost painful sharpness out of the ache that
possessed her.

There had never been a time when she had ever
felt anything like this, she acknowledged dizzily,
when she had felt so—so driven, so—so in need,
so helplessly out of control.

She shivered as Guard released her nipple and
the air struck coolly against her hot, damp flesh.

In the soft light, she looked down at Guard's dark
head, still bent over her body as he kissed the hollow
between her breasts and then moved lower.

Her own flesh looked so alien to her. Her breasts
swollen...flushed—the one Guard had caressed still
engorged, still aching...

She tensed as his tongue circled her navel, her body clenching.

Guard's hand had left her stomach and was resting on her outer thigh, sliding beneath her to lift her so that——

Now she did protest, her eyes wild with shock at the sight of Guard's dark head between her thighs, his fingers dark against her so much paler skin as he lifted her body effortlessly, arranging it, imprisoning it in a position of such intimacy that Rosy could feel herself flushing. But she still couldn't drag her gaze away from the sight of his dark head bent over the most vulnerable, sacred part of her body.

When his lips brushed the soft flesh of her inner thigh, Rosy shivered uncontrollably, self-consciousness forgotten in the tide of sensation that flooded through her.

Guard was still kissing and caressing her skin, moving closer to the most sensitive part of her.

Even before he got there, her body was responding to him, aware of him, wanting him, ignoring the shocked demands of her mind that it abandon such wantonness.

Heat poured through her as she heard the thick, pleasured sound Guard gave when he discovered how femalely responsive she was to him—how welcome was the delicate touch of his tongue against the small nub of flesh so sensitive to his caress that Rosy's whole body was gripped by the paroxysm of aching pleasure that shot through her.

She knew Guard must have felt it too, because his hands suddenly tensed on her body and he raised

his head to look at her, the skin along his cheekbones drawn taut and burning darkly with heat.

The look he gave her made her heart slowly
somersault.

'No,' she protested huskily, as Guard bent his
head back to her body.

'Yes,' he insisted thickly, telling her, 'Have you
any idea what doing this feels like? How addictive
the taste of you is, how much I've wanted you like
this? You're right, Rosy,' he said roughly. 'You're
a woman—wholly, completely and utterly so.'

Rosy shuddered in silent ecstasy as his mouth re-
found her.

This time the pleasure was different because this
time her body and her senses were prepared... knew. She held her breath as she felt the
exquisite agony of anticipation build up inside her,
releasing it on a sharp, aching cry of release as the
pleasure engulfed her, sweeping her up in its
roaring, leaping, flooding tide.

'Guard, now, now...please... I want you inside
me now.'

She cried out the words almost without knowing
she was saying them, knowing only that there was
a small part of her that still ached... that still
needed, that felt empty and unfulfilled, and that
the only thing that could satisfy it was the feel of
Guard's body within her, the sensation of him
moving deep inside her. She felt him slowly release
her, separating himself from her, smoothing away
the bedclothes from her body and then kneeling
back from her.

As he moved her breath caught in her throat. In the dim light she had seen the full power of his body—how aroused he was, how male.

'Say that again,' he demanded. 'Tell me again that you want me.'

She should have been intimidated into desire-stifling, shy self-consciousness by the way he was looking at her, by the roughly aroused tone of his voice, but instead...

Instead she felt a power, a knowledge she had never known she could possess and, instead of flinching coyly beneath his regard, Rosy held his gaze, stretching her body with languorous sensuality, parting her legs, her spine arching slightly in subtle, sensual invitation as she told him huskily, 'I want you, Guard. I want you now... please, now... now.'

She moaned in eager excitement as his hands slid up over her body, his touch, his gaze, his arousal showing his response to her.

As his hands cupped her breasts he leaned over her and kissed her mouth slowly, with gentle precision, and then she reached up to him and wound her arms round him, pulling him down against her with fierce, demanding desire.

'Is this what you want, Rosy...? This...?' he demanded urgently as he held her, touched her, filled her with the full power of his body.

'Yes. Yes. Yes...' Rosy told him compulsively as she clung to him and urged him physically and vocally to thrust even deeper within her.

'You're so small,' Guard protested unsteadily. 'So——'

'I want you,' Rosy repeated. 'Please, Guard, please... I want all of you...'

She felt his body shudder as he tried to resist her and failed.

The sensation of his moving so gently and so deeply within her filled her with female joy and triumph. Her body, unlike his, might be untutored in such intimacy but it had its own power, its own strength, the strength to sustain the fierce maleness of Guard's release and to match it.

Against her body she could feel the intense drumbeat of Guard's heart starting to slow down slightly. His arms were wrapped around her as he held her tightly against him, his skin damp with sweat, like her own.

Now that the need, the desire which had driven her was sated, she suddenly felt very shy and unsure of herself.

Held fast in thrall to her physical and emotional yearnings, she had known only that she loved Guard and that she wanted him. And that he had wanted her. But now, suddenly, the enormity of those emotions evoked a sharp fear within her. Loving Guard was such a new concept for her. Wanting him—needing him—with so much passion and intensity made her feel very vulnerable.

She felt his lips brush her cheek in a light caress, his breath warm against her mouth. Panic overwhelmed her. Quickly she turned her head away, aware of the tension in his body as he withdrew slightly from her to look down at her.

'Rosy! What...'

Rosy rushed nervously into speech, unsure if she wanted to hear what Guard might be going to say.

'Well, at least now Edward isn't going to be able to claim that our marriage isn't legal.'

She felt Guard's body stiffen.

'Is that what all this was about?' he demanded curtly, withdrawing completely from her. 'Is that why——?' As he swore under his breath, Rosy flinched. 'My God...and I actually thought——'

'Guard?' Rosy questioned uncertainly, but he wasn't listening to her, he wasn't even looking at her, she recognised unhappily as he moved over to the empty side of the bed and snapped off the light.

Keeping his back towards her, he told her grimly. 'Go to sleep, Rosy. Just go to sleep...'

Miserably, Rosy curled her body into a small, tight ball. Her body ached slightly in unfamiliar places, her throat felt tight with tears and, ridiculously, after the wanton way in which she had begged Guard to make love to her, much as she longed to do so, she couldn't bring herself to tell him how much, how very much she needed now to be held and reassured by him, to be told that he understood how she felt, that he knew how difficult it was for her to come to terms with the reality of her feelings for him...her love.

The words trembled on her lips and were suppressed as her eyes burned with hot tears.

Perhaps Guard wasn't holding her...reassuring her...because what had happened between them didn't mean the same to him. Because he *didn't* feel the same way about her as she did about him.

Men *were* like that about sex, weren't they? They could enjoy it without feeling any emotional involvement with the woman concerned.

But he *must* know how she felt. He must have recognised what had happened to her. After all, he knew her views on casual sex, he knew she would never—*could* never—give herself so completely to a man without... without loving him.

As the tears started to roll down her face, she bit down hard on her bottom lip to stop herself from making any noise.

Cautiously, Rosy opened her eyes, but it was all right. She was alone in the bed, alone in the room, apparently.

She sat up slowly, hugging the bedclothes protectively round her body, her face flushing as she recognised the cause of the slight ache deep within her body.

'You're so small,' Guard had said, but the deep, compulsive thrusting of his body within her own hadn't hurt her at all—in fact, the ache she felt now...

Caution was replaced by wistful longing as she looked at the empty space in the bed next to her.

Last night she had been silly to let Guard turn away from her without telling him how she felt; today things would be different, she told herself optimistically. But where was Guard?

She pushed back the bedclothes and then frowned as she remembered that she didn't have any clean clothes. She would have to put on her worn ones and go down to her bedroom. Her frown deepened as her gaze focused on a neat pile of white underclothes on one of the bedroom chairs. Her underclothes.

Someone, and it could only have been Guard, had anticipated her need. A small smile started to curl her mouth.

Guard was quite right, she decided half an hour later as she emerged from the bathroom, showered and dressed. Her girlish nightshirts were not really the thing for a married woman, and oh, so totally unnecessary when she had Guard next to her in bed to keep her warm.

A nightshirt, or indeed any other kind of nightwear, was not only unnecessary but unwelcome as well when it came between her and the sensual warmth of Guard's skin, the touch of his hands and mouth, when——

Shakily Rosy tried to banish her wantonly erotic thoughts, but as she glanced in the mirror she suspected that her flushed face and shining eyes gave her away.

When Guard saw her, would he immediately be reminded of last night? Would he perhaps suggest that they come back upstairs and——?

Dizzily, Rosy opened the bedroom door and hurried towards the stairs. She had never imagined that loving someone would make her so physically aroused or so responsive, but then Guard was so very, very special. She drew in a small, ecstatically happy breath, her whole body glowing with pleasure and love.

As Rosy got to the bottom of the stairs, Mrs Frinton came out of the library.

'Where's Guard?' Rosy asked her eagerly, a happy anticipatory smile already curling her mouth.

Mrs Frinton looked slightly perplexed by Rosy's question, as though it had surprised her.

'He's gone out, Miss Rosy,' she told her. 'He said to let you sleep in as you'd had a disturbed night and to tell you that he wouldn't be back until late this evening. Something about having dinner with an important client in London.'

Rosy's face fell, her earlier joy turning to bewilderment.

Why hadn't Guard woken her, said something? How could he leave her like that after last night, without a word? Without any kind of acknowledgement of what had happened? The day suddenly yawned emptily ahead of her, full of hours which would drag slowly past while she waited for Guard's return.

'Can I get you some breakfast?' Mrs Frinton offered.

Silently, Rosy shook her head, swallowing back the hard lump blocking her throat.

Ten minutes later she was on her own in the library, standing staring disconsolately out of the window when the door opened. For a moment, she thought it was Guard, her spirits lifting, a welcoming smile warming her mouth as she turned round. But it wasn't Guard who was walking into the room, it was Edward.

'No Guard?' Edward commented. 'Well, don't say I didn't try to warn you. You do realise why he married you, don't you, Rosy?'

Go away, Edward, Rosy wanted to tell him, but the words were stuck in her throat. Instead, she turned her head away from him, trying to silence him by ignoring him, but Edward simply laughed unkindly.

'Don't want to hear the truth, is that it? Can't face up to it? Well, my dear Rosy, I'm afraid we all have to face up to unpleasant things from time to time. I found it extremely unpleasant, for instance, learning that I wasn't going to inherit this place.'

'You knew the terms of Grandfather's will,' Rosy told him unsteadily.

'Oh, yes, indeed,' Edward agreed nastily. 'And I wasn't the only person who knew then, was I, Rosy? Weren't you the *least* little bit suspicious when Guard proposed to you? He's known you long enough, after all. If he'd really wanted you he'd have——'

'I don't have to listen to any of this, Edward,' Rosy protested angrily. 'Guard's and my feelings, our marriage, are private. They don't have anything to do with you.'

'Oh, yes, they do,' Edward contradicted her bitterly. 'Grow up, Rosy, and face facts. He married you for one reason and one reason only. He married you for Queen's Meadow, but he won't really be secure here until he's got you pregnant, will he? Until he's sure that his child will inherit. What's wrong, Rosy?' Edward taunted her. 'Surely you didn't really think that the reason he's so keen to take you to bed is because he wants *you*? Grow up. If he'd wanted you that badly, he'd have had you years ago,' he told her crudely, while Rosy gasped in shocked, distraught protest, all the colour leaving her face, and Edward reinforced his cruelty by adding, 'Why should a man like him want you? He could have any woman he wanted—any woman...

'I don't want to hurt you, Rosy,' Edward lied, abruptly changing tack, his voice becoming nauseatingly soft and wheedling. 'I'm just trying to help you, protect you. You could leave him now, before it's too late. Show him that you've seen through him. How can you stay with him, after all, knowing that he doesn't really want you? You *know* that he doesn't want you, don't you, Rosy? If he did, he'd be here with you, wouldn't he? Do you even know where he is or who he's with?'

Rosy daren't turn round and confront Edward. If she did he would see the hurt in her eyes.

Guard *had* married her for Queen's Meadow. Of course he had... She knew that—had known it all along. How on earth could she have been so stupid to believe otherwise?

'Edward, have you got a minute? I can't seem to find my car keys.'

Rosy's body sagged with relief as she heard Margaret's timid voice from the doorway.

She could hear Edward's irritable, carping voice as he followed his wife out into the hallway. Was it really only last night that she had been pitying Margaret for being married to a man who so obviously didn't love her, wondering how on earth she could bear to stay married to him? How blindly and foolishly she had tempted fate. What was it the Greeks had called fate's swift reprisal for such temerity? Nemesis, that was it... Nemesis.

Well, Guard was most definitely her nemesis. Guard and her helpless, pathetic, unwanted love for him.

Guard *didn't* love her and she had been a fool ever to think he did—or that he could.

Just because *her* feelings for him had changed so dramatically, that didn't mean that his for her had undergone a similar metamorphosis.

But he *had* made love to her, held her, touched her, caressed her and taken her to the heights of ecstasy and held her there...

A small sob forced its way past her lips.

Because she had begged him to, pleaded with him to. He was a man, after all, with a very potent male sex drive.

How could she have been so stupid? And how could she ever face him again now, knowing...? Thank God Edward had inadvertently made her realise the truth before she had actually told Guard that she loved him.

She gulped painfully. At least her pride would still be intact, even if her heart wasn't.

If Guard said anything to her about what had happened, she would simply have to pretend that it had been the result of her fear, her panic that Edward might discover the truth.

CHAPTER TEN

'ROSY.'

Rosy tensed as she heard Guard calling her name. She had almost reached the front door; could she possibly open it and escape? He was back early anyway. In the month they had been married he had worked late virtually every evening. She herself had planned to be out when he came in, just as she had been every evening this last week.

It had been a godsend when Ralph had asked her if she could possibly switch shifts with one of the other voluntary workers. She had not only agreed, she had opted to work several extra evenings as well.

She had seen the way Ralph frowned as he asked her, 'Are you sure? Won't Guard object?'

'Guard's very busy himself,' Rosy had told him truthfully. Very busy with his work, or very busy avoiding her?

Her mouth curled in a small, bitterly painful smile. It seemed like a lifetime ago now since she had so naïvely worried about having to share a bed with Guard.

Then, when he had teased her about the effects of his proximity on her libido, it had never occurred to her just how prophetic his words might turn out to be. Why should it? She had been so unaware then, so unknowing.

Now... with Edward and Margaret still in the house they had no option but to continue to share

a bedroom and a bed, but Guard always took care
to make sure he stayed downstairs until she was
asleep, or until he thought she was asleep and, out
of pride, Rosy obligingly went along with the deceit.
Lying there, with her eyes closed while he moved
about the bedroom and the bathroom, trying desperately to hold at bay the feelings, the needs, the
emotions that were causing her so much pain.

Not even when she was sure that Guard himself
was asleep did she allow herself the luxury of tears.
She dared not. If Guard should wake up and find
her crying . . .

Once or twice in the week after that night, she
had been aware of him watching her and, on several
occasions, she had sensed that he was going to say
something about what had happened, but each time
her own fear of what he might actually be going to
say caused her to evade the subject.

The worst time had been the night after they had
made love.

Rosy had gone to bed early, knowing that there
was no way she could possibly sleep, and knowing
as well that there was no way that she could stay
downstairs with Guard.

She had been pretending to be asleep when he
came into the bedroom, but she had obviously not
deceived him, because he came over to her and told
her softly, 'I know you're awake, Rosy. We have
to talk.'

'No,' she had denied in panic, guessing what it
was he wanted to say. He wanted to tell her that he
had guessed how much she loved him but that he
did not love her. He wanted to remind her of the
terms of their marriage, to shatter the illusion of

their lovemaking that she was clinging on to so desperately by telling her that, to him, it had been nothing other than a mere sexual encounter, that the emotion, the intensity, the closeness and commitment she had felt had all been fabricated by her own imagination and need.

'No... I don't want to talk,' she had told him fiercely, adding childishly, 'There isn't anything to talk about.'

She had tensed a little as she saw the muscle beating angrily in his jaw, but he hadn't argued with her or pressed the matter, simply saying heavily, 'Very well, Rosy, if that's what you really want.'

She hadn't responded. How could she? Instead, she had turned her face away from him as he walked away from her, curling herself into a small, miserable ball. What she really wanted was *him*—his love, his loving. What she really wanted was for him to take her in his arms and tell her that he loved her, that he wanted her, that he couldn't and wouldn't live without her.

'Rosy,' Guard called again, his voice ominously sharp.

It was too late for her to take flight now, Rosy recognised; he was already in the hall.

'What is it, Guard?' she asked him, without looking directly at him. 'I was just on my way out. I'm working at the shelter this evening. I must go, otherwise I'm going to be late.'

'No,' Guard told her softly. 'Tonight you're not working *anywhere*, Rosy. Tonight you and I are going to talk.'

'But I can't let Ralph down.' Rosy panicked. 'He's expecting me and they're already short-staffed because of all these meetings Ralph's been having about renewing the lease.'

Their landlord at the shelter had recently announced that he intended to sell the building when the lease ran out. Ralph was trying to find a way of raising enough money for them to buy the building themselves, but so far he had not had much luck. He had even asked to suggest to Guard that he buy the building for them.

'No. I can't do that, Ralph,' Rosy had told him uncomfortably.

And nor could she provide the money herself, since her capital was all tied up in various trusts.

'We can talk tomorrow,' she suggested now.

'Can we?' Guard asked her sardonically. 'Are you sure that by the time tomorrow comes you won't have found something far more important to do? No, Rosy. I'm not the most patient of men at the best of times but, given the situation, I accept that things aren't easy for you. But running away never solved anything, you know.

'When you and I married, we made a bargain and that bargain was that, as far as anyone else was concerned, our marriage would appear perfectly normal. It isn't normal, Rosy, for a couple who've only been married a month to spend so little time together, especially when one of that couple makes it plain that she——'

'*You're* the one who's always working late,' Rosy interrupted him dangerously.

'Am I? And how would you know what time I come home, Rosy, since you're never here?'

Rosy stared at him. She knew because Edward had taken good care to make sure that she did, never missing an opportunity to comment pointedly on the fact that Guard had not arrived home until gone eight or nine and, certainly when Rosy returned home from her shift at the shelter after eleven, he was invariably shut in the library still working.

'We made a bargain,' Guard repeated grimly. 'But *you* aren't making any attempt to keep your side of it, are you? You'd rather spend all your time at the shelter.'

'It seemed the best thing to do,' Rosy told him woodenly.

'What? Best? Best for whom?' Guard demanded savagely. 'People are starting to talk,' he warned her. 'They're starting to wonder what kind of marriage we have, what kind of relationship when we're spending so much time apart. My God, I've even had Edward offering me commiseration and advice, warning me that people are beginning to comment about the amount of time you're spending with Ralph. Edward also seems to think that Ralph might have tried to persuade you to help finance the shelter.'

'Is that—is that what you wanted to talk to me about?' Rosy asked jerkily, warily.

'One of the things,' Guard agreed.

One of them? What were the others? Rosy wondered miserably. Only yesterday Edward had commented on how unhappy she looked; 'lovelorn' was the word he had used to describe her, pseudo-sympathetically pretending to feel sorry for her because Guard was neglecting her.

'You mustn't wear your heart on your sleeve so obviously,' he had advised her. 'Men like Guard enjoy the chase, the hunt. You've made it all far too easy for him, Rosy, and now he's bored.'

'*Has* Ralph asked you for money, Rosy?' Guard asked her sternly.

'He's worried about the lease, about losing the premises,' Rosy responded indirectly. 'The shelter needs——'

'The shelter needs...' Guard interrupted her angrily. 'Tell me something, Rosy, do you ever think about any other needs? Anyone else's needs? Or are you really so blind that——?'

He broke off as the door opened and Edward walked into the hall.

'Sorry,' he apologised insincerely, his foxy eyes flicking from Rosy's pale face to Guard's angry one and back again. 'Have I interrupted a bad moment?'

'Did you want something, Edward?' Guard asked him irritably, without taking his eyes off Rosy's face, ignoring his question.

'Yes, if you don't mind, Guard, I wanted to have a word with you. The boys will be home from school soon and Margaret's fussing about the lack of proper fire-escape facilities on the upper floor and I must say I have to agree with her. For safety's sake, I really think we ought to move down a floor while they're here...'

Quickly, Rosy headed for the door, ignoring Guard's sharply commanding, 'Rosy...wait...'

Half expecting that he would come after her, she almost ran to her car, her hands shaking as she unlocked the door and got in.

'We have to talk', he had said, but she couldn't. She was far too afraid of what he might say, of hearing him tell her that he had had enough, that he was leaving.

And yet, really, wouldn't that be for the best? How long could she go on living so close to him, knowing how much she loved him, knowing that Edward was watching their every movement, knowing that her time with him was steadily trickling away, living in dread of betraying her feelings and having to bear the pain of hearing him say that he didn't want her love...?

All evening at the shelter, she was anxious and on edge, unable to concentrate properly on what she was doing, and it was a relief when her shift finally came to an end and she was free to go home.

The first thing she noticed as she parked her car outside the house was that Guard's car was missing.

Her heart took a forlorn dive into misery, even though she tried to tell herself that it was just as well that he wasn't there.

Her head had been aching all evening, and she was in the kitchen taking a couple of aspirin when Edward walked in.

'Not feeling very well?' he asked her sharply.

'I've got a headache,' Rosy responded listlessly. She hated the habit he had of always appearing when she least wanted him to, it was almost eerie, intimidating, as though he was secretly spying on her.

'Guard's gone out,' he told her, watching her.

'Yes, I realise that,' Rosy agreed tonelessly.

She wanted to leave the kitchen but Edward was standing right in front of her, almost physically barring her way.

'He had a telephone call—from a woman,' Edward told her with relish. 'He said to tell you that he'd be away all night.'

Rosy felt the blood drain from her face, and knew that Edward had witnessed her body's reaction to her emotions.

'Oh, poor Rosy, you have got it badly, haven't you?' Edward sympathised insincerely. 'But you can't win, you know. Sooner or later he's going to leave you. Oh, he'll stay long enough to make sure of this place, but he's already getting bored with you, isn't he? A young woman of your age, he probably expected to get you pregnant straight away... *Are* you pregnant, Rosy? You've been looking very pale recently...'

Rosy gasped in outraged anger.

'That's none of your business,' she told him fiercely.

'Oh, yes, it is,' Edward responded softly. 'It's very much my business. Just as this house is very much my business. I hope you aren't pregnant, Rosy, because if you are... Well, let's just say that in a house like this there are all kinds of hazards for a woman in a delicate condition, if you take my meaning. Guard wouldn't be very pleased if you lost his baby, would he, Rosy? All that time wasted. The boring job of having to do it all again to be faced, when he would obviously so much rather spend his time with someone else... You've only been married a month and already he's bored with you, Rosy. Leave him now, while there's still time.

He only wants the house. He doesn't want you. He's never wanted you.'

With a small sob, Rosy managed to push her way past her tormentor, almost running out of the kitchen as she headed for the stairs and the security of her bedroom.

The security? How could she feel secure here now, after what Edward had just said, the threats he had just made?

He must be mad, deranged—but Rosy knew that he wasn't. She shivered violently as she curled up in the middle of the bed.

How would she feel right now if she had actually been carrying Guard's child? The cold sickness, the fear, the anguish, the protective way her hand instinctively covered her stomach told her the answer.

She couldn't go on like this, loving Guard, wanting him, knowing he didn't love her, living in fear of Edward and his threats.

But where else could she go? The shelter? A wryly bitter smile curled her mouth at the thought... Hardly.

'You're not eating your breakfast.'

'I'm not hungry,' Rosy responded wanly to Guard's terse comment. It was Saturday morning and for once he had no serious business to take him out of the house.

Nothing had been said about her refusal to agree to talk to him, and no explanation given to her for his absence all night earlier in the week.

Guard was just pushing his chair back from the table and standing up when Edward walked into the breakfast-room.

'I've got to go out later,' Guard told her distantly. 'I don't know how long I'll be away. What are your plans?'

'I've—I've got some shopping to do later,' Rosy fibbed, avoiding looking at him, her whole body tensing as she felt him looking at her.

'Ah, these modern marriages,' Edward quipped, smiling at them.

He wasn't smiling an hour later as he caught up with Rosy on the stairs, just after Guard had gone out.

'Stop making it hard for yourself, Rosy,' he advised her. 'Leave him. He's making it very obvious how little he thinks of you—and how much he thinks of her.'

'Her?'

The betraying, agonised word had escaped before Rosy could silence it.

'Oh, come on.' Edward smirked. 'You can't be that naïve. Your husband stays away all night; there can only be one reason, can't there? There's got to be someone else, hasn't there, Rosy? Several someone elses if Guard's reputation is anything to go by.'

Suddenly, Rosy had had enough. She could feel the tears filling her eyes and threatening to spill down her face. All Edward's barbed pinpricks, all his cruelty, all his threats, all the pain and misery of loving Guard and knowing she wasn't loved in return suddenly became too much for her.

Head down, she turned and fled to the sanctuary of the bedroom.

The bedroom—*their* bedroom—the room and the bed she shared with Guard.

Shared with him. She squeezed her eyes tightly closed against the hot, betraying flood of her tears.

As the scalding tears burned their way down her face, she reached out helplessly for Guard's pillow, wrapping her arms round it and burying her face in it, trying to absorb the faintly lingering scent of him into her own body, as though it were a drug which could ease her pain.

'Rosy...Rosy, what is it? What are you doing up here?'

Guard. But he had gone out. Rosy tensed as she heard his voice, not daring to turn round.

'What's wrong?' Guard asked. 'Aren't you feeling well? Rosy, answer me...'

He was standing next to the bed now, leaning over her, his hand reaching out towards her. Miserably, Rosy lifted her face out of his pillow.

'You're crying?'

He sat down on the bed next to her. Next to her, but still apart from her, Rosy noticed.

'What is it? What's wrong?'

'Nothing,' Rosy lied.

'Is it Ralph? The shelter? Have you...?'

Ralph? Rosy stared at him. Why should she be crying over Ralph?

'Ralph! Of course it isn't,' she denied fretfully.

There was a look in Guard's eyes which made her heart suddenly start to thud unsteadily.

'Well, if it's not Ralph then what, or rather who, is it?' Guard persisted quietly.

Edgily, Rosy sat up and moved slightly away from him.

'I thought you had to go out,' she told him.

'That can wait,' Guard responded flatly. 'This can't. What is it, Rosy? And don't tell me nothing. The day "nothing" makes *you* cry...'

To Rosy's consternation, he suddenly reached out and touched her hot, damp face in a gesture which could almost be mistaken for tenderness, just as the look in his eyes could almost be mistaken for real, genuine concern. But that would be a fatal mistake for her to make, she warned herself, another fatal mistake.

She couldn't tell him the truth. How could she, when——? She tensed abruptly as she heard someone walking down the corridor.

'It's Edward, Guard,' she exclaimed in panic. 'Don't let him come in. Don't——'

'Edward?'

As she heard the sharp query in Guard's voice, Rosy's face flooded with betraying colour.

'Is it *Edward* who's the cause of this...these?' Guard demanded, his fingers brushing gently against her face.

Rosy bit down on her bottom lip, not trusting herself to answer, but she couldn't stop the hot, sad flow of tears that gave away her real feelings.

'Tell me,' Guard commanded her. 'All of it, Rosy,' he warned her. 'I want to know what the hell's been going on. What the hell he's done to cause this.'

'I can't,' Rosy protested miserably. 'Please don't make me, Guard. I just wish he would go away,' she wept. 'I hate having him watching me, spying on me. He knows, Guard. I know he does and he——'

'He knows what?'

'That this isn't a real marriage . . . a proper marriage,' Rosy told him. 'He keeps telling me—threatening me——'

'Threatening you?' Guard interrupted her sharply. 'Rosy, there's nothing he can do to either of us now,' he told her. 'Surely you must have realised that. No matter what the reasons were for our marrying, what our intentions were concerning the reality of that marriage, Edward's power to damage us was totally destroyed the night you and I turned our marriage from a fiction to a reality. There's nothing he can do now, no legal recourse open to him.'

'No—no legal one,' Rosy agreed tiredly.

Guard frowned at her.

'Rosy, what is it . . . ? What are you trying to say?'

She was shivering now, her body suddenly very cold; she felt ill almost, like someone suffering from a very bad virus.

'Rosy!' Guard warned her.

Wearily, Rosy shook her head.

'He keeps saying I should end our marriage,' she told him quietly. 'He thinks you're trying to . . . He thinks . . .' Flushing, she ducked her head, unable to bring herself to look at him as she told him unsteadily, 'He thinks that if you and I have a child that your claim to the house will be more secure. He's guessed that that's why you married me, Guard. He even threatened——' She swallowed hard and gave a small, hard laugh. 'He told me that—that in a house like this it would be very easy for a woman to lose her baby . . .'

'*What?*'

Rosy winced as she heard the fury in Guard's voice.

'Stay here,' he told her.

He was gone less than half an hour and when he came back, the controlled, totally blanked-off expression in his eyes made Rosy feel afraid.

What had he said to Edward and, even more important, what had Edward said to him? Had he told Guard about her feelings? Had he——?

'Edward's gone, Rosy,' Guard told her flatly. 'And he won't be coming back.'

Rosy stared at him. How on earth had Guard managed to make him leave so easily and so quickly? Edward had been like a limpet in his determination to stay, and Guard had told her that there was too much risk involved in insisting that he left.

'He's gone? Just like that?'

Fresh tears rolled down her face, but this time they were tears of relief.

'Oh, God, Rosy. Rosy, don't cry...'

Rosy tensed as Guard moved towards her, obviously intending to take hold of her and comfort her, flinching back from him, her eyes wide and dark with distress.

'There's no need to back away from me as though I'm some kind of—— I'm not going to touch you.'

'No, I know you aren't,' Rosy agreed woodenly, looking hurriedly away from him as she felt fresh tears starting to fall.

'Well, if you know that, then why on earth——?' she heard Guard saying. 'Rosy,' he demanded softly, his voice suddenly changing. 'Rosy, look at me.'

'I can't,' Rosy whispered. 'I can't.'

'Yes, you can.'

She trembled as Guard's hand cupped her face, gently tilting it upwards so that he could look into her tear-drenched eyes.

'Now,' he told her quietly, 'if you *know* I'm not going to touch you, then why flinch away from me like that?'

Rosy blinked hard, trying to suppress her tears, her lips trembling as she failed and the full force of her emotions stormed through her, shattering her defences.

'It's because I *want* you to touch me,' she told him in a tormented, husky voice. 'Because I love you and I want you and I can't bear—— Guard . . . Guard . . .'

Her protest was smothered beneath his mouth as he reached out for her, holding her so tightly that she could feel the fierce beat of his heart as though it were her own.

'Rosy . . . Rosy.'

She scarcely recognised the stifled, intense voice as Guard's, the fiercely whispered endearments, the hungry, passionate kisses. Surely she must be imagining them, she thought dizzily.

Surely this *couldn't* really be Guard, holding her like this, kissing her mouth, her face, her throat . . . Telling her how much he loved her, how much he had always loved her, telling her he had waited for what felt like half his life, her lifetime, to hear her say what she had just said.

'But you can't love me,' Rosy protested shakily, pushing him slightly away from her and looking up into his eyes, her own shy and bewildered. 'You've always disliked me—hated me.'

'Oh, Rosy,' Guard groaned. 'Only *you* could think that. Only you *do* think that. Why the hell do you think I married you?'

Rosy frowned.

'Because I asked you to. Because you wanted the house.'

'No, Rosy,' Guard corrected her thickly. 'I wanted *you*. Did want, have wanted, do want, will want,' he stressed, ticking each assertion off on her fingers, pausing to kiss each one of them tenderly and then less tenderly as he saw the expression in her eyes.

Rosy felt her whole body jerk in shocked reaction to the sensation of his sucking on her fingertips.

She could feel what he was doing to her right down to her toes. And everywhere else as well.

'But you didn't *want* to marry me. I had to ask you,' she reminded him in a small voice. 'And you said you needed time...'

'Time to get myself under control and work out just how capable I was of going along with what you were asking. You were damn lucky I didn't snatch you up there and then and take you to bed, just to show you exactly what I thought of your plans for our business marriage. Perhaps that's what I should have done,' he added, lifting his head to look at her.

Rosy couldn't conceal the sharp *frisson* of excitement that ran through her, or the hot colour burning her skin.

'*Would* you have liked that, Rosy?' Guard asked her thickly, letting her see just how much her reaction was affecting him, exciting him, Rosy recognised, on a small wobble of uncertain delight. 'Would you have liked it if I'd carried you off to bed and made love to you?'

'I... Oh, Guard, how can you possibly have loved me without my knowing?' Rosy demanded giddily.

'With extreme frustration,' Guard told her drily, 'and a hell of a lot of jealousy.'

'You, jealous? Of whom?'

'Ralph, for one,' Guard told her quietly. 'And Bressée for another. My God, when I saw the way you were letting him flirt with you... I've always considered myself a very logical and cautious human being, but that night... I wanted to take you to bed and stamp the seal of my possession on you so clearly that no man—no man—would ever doubt that you were mine.'

'Edward said you didn't love me. That you just wanted the house,' Rosy told him painfully. 'He said—he said you had someone else and I thought... Why, if you love me, Guard, did you...? Didn't you...?' She stopped and looked pleadingly at him. 'Why didn't you say something that night, the night...?'

'Oh, Rosy. How little you know,' Guard told her, but his derisive look was, Rosy recognised, more for himself than for her. 'I was angry with myself for—for letting things get out of hand, for letting my feelings, my needs, destroy my self-control.

You'd turned to me for comfort—in fear and panic.
I never intended...I thought you must have guessed
how I felt and that was why you refused to talk
about what had happened.'

'I thought you were angry with me,' Rosy whispered. 'In the morning when I woke up and you
weren't there...'

'I thought you wouldn't want me to be there.'

Rosy gave him an uncertain look.

'But you must have known. You must have
guessed that I——'

'That you what? Responded passionately to me?
Yes, I knew that, but then you've always been
passionately intense about everything you've done.'

'But I begged you to make love to me,' Rosy reminded him, half-ashamed. 'I...'

'You told me you wanted me, but I dared not let
myself believe that that was anything more than the
impulse of the moment, a reaction brought on by
the trauma of what you were enduring. And then,
of course, I also had my guilt to deal with.'

'Your guilt? For making love to me?' Rosy asked
him, frowning.

'Among other things,' he agreed.

'What other things,' Rosy demanded, perplexed.

'Agreeing to marry you instead of trying to help
you find some other way round the problem,' he
told her, watching her face carefully. 'Taking advantage of Edward's decision to move in here...'

'Taking advantage? In what way?'

Guard looked at her and then at the bed.

'In the way that led to your and my becoming
lovers. Do you honestly think I couldn't have gone

and got your clothes for you if I'd really wanted to, Rosy?'

'But you didn't want to sleep with me. You said so,' Rosy protested.

'Oh, Rosy,' Guard groaned. 'Of course I wanted to sleep with you. I wanted to sleep with you, touch and kiss you, love you. I wanted it all and more—much, much more. I wanted you to hold me, to touch me, to want me. To love me,' he told her huskily.

He cupped her face and looked down into her eyes.

'Do you really believe I couldn't have found some way of getting rid of Edward, some way of ensuring that we didn't have to share a room, if that was really what I'd wanted? Have I shocked you?'

Rosy shook her head.

'Surprised me,' she admitted. 'I had no idea.'

'I think I fell in love with you the night I found you poaching,' Guard told her softly. 'Grubby, undersized, very angry—a little girl, still, in so many ways and yet in so many others very, very much a woman. Or at least that was what my emotions and my body told me. My mind...' He shook his head.

'I knew it was too soon. You were too young. You didn't even like me. But then you went on not liking me—not liking me but reacting so emotionally to me that I couldn't stop myself from clinging to the hope that maybe...just maybe——'

'I'd fall in love with you,' Rosy broke in softly.

'Is that what's happened, Rosy?' he asked her quietly.

Rosy shook her head. 'No, I haven't fallen in love with you, Guard,' she told him firmly, lifting her hand to his face in an instinctive gesture of comfort as she saw his pain. 'Falling in love is for teenagers, girls. I'm a woman. I love you, Guard,' she told him emotionally. 'I love you as a woman loves a man—wholly, completely, for ever.'

She trembled as she saw the moisture in his eyes, reaching up to pull him down against her, whispering to him, 'Oh, Guard... Guard...'

Some time later, lying naked in his arms, watching as he reached out his hand to cup her breast, reluctant, it seemed, even now to release her, she smiled lovingly at him.

His thumb stroked the tip of her nipple, swollen still from their earlier lovemaking.

'Were you really jealous of Ralph?' she marvelled.

'Extremely,' Guard responded wryly. 'A fact which Edward played on to very good effect.'

'He manipulated us both,' Rosy acknowledged. 'What did you say to him to make him leave, Guard?' she asked him.

Guard's head paused in its descent towards her breast. 'I told him that if he ever, ever said or did anything to upset you again, I'd make him regret it for the rest of his life. I also told him that if he wasn't out of the house and out of our lives within half an hour he'd find his financial and business affairs under the kind of scrutiny that would make the Fraud Squad look tame.'

His mouth opened gently over her nipple.

'Mmm...' Rosy closed her eyes, stretching her body luxuriously beneath his caress. 'I thought you'd——'

'What?' Guard asked her throatily, releasing her nipple to smile into her arousal-darkened eyes. His hand stroked the satin-soft skin of her thigh, his own eyes darkening as she made a small, soft sound of pleasure.

'Is there something else you'd rather be doing?' he suggested.

'No... nothing,' Rosy denied, unsteadily.

Guard's mouth returned to her nipple, caressing it with such slow deliberation that it was almost a torment.

'How would you like it if I did that to you?' she protested as her body started to tremble with arousal.

'Try me,' Guard invited her.

For a moment she thought he was joking, but then she realised that he meant it.

Shyly and a little uncertainly at first, she touched the soft-haired flesh of his chest with her lips, slowly moving closer to his flat male nipple.

The sensation of taking it into her mouth was unexpectedly erotic, so much more so than she had anticipated that it made her tense slightly and hesitate.

'No, Rosy... Don't stop...don't stop,' she heard Guard groan thickly as his hands came up and held her head against his body. She could feel his fingers trembling slightly against her scalp, feel the fierce, fast beat of his heart, the arousal of his body as it responded to her hesitant suckling.

If touching him like this gave him so much pleasure, then how much more pleasure could she give him by caressing him with the same kind of intimacy he had shown her?

She almost started to ask him, but then stopped. There were some things, she decided quietly, that a woman needed to discover for herself.

He didn't say anything when she touched his thigh, nor when she placed some light butterfly kisses over his belly, but she could feel his tension, feel it in his sudden almost painful grip on her wrist as she moved down his body.

He didn't try to restrain her, but he didn't encourage her either, and for a moment Rosy almost changed her mind.

What if he didn't want her to...? Didn't like...? But *she* wanted to, she recognised, on a sudden sharp ache of desire. She wanted to touch him, taste him, know him with the same intimacy with which he knew her.

The musky, male scent of his body made her own ache sharply. She could feel his tension as she slowly slid her mouth down over him, touching him with her tongue, delicately exploring him, startled by the surge of pleasure that what she was doing gave her, the immediate and now easily recognised reaction of her flesh to what she had always naïvely assumed was a caress that sexually pleased only the recipient and not the giver.

Guard's hand fell away from her wrist as a deep shudder racked his body. Beneath her fingertips the muscles in his thigh were tense.

'Rosy... Oh, God, Rosy... No more. No more,' she heard him protest in a stifled voice as she continued to caress him. His hands gripped her shoulders and his body writhed fiercely as he almost dragged her up the bed.

'Didn't you like it?' Rosy asked him uncertainly as he buried his mouth in her throat.

'Like it...?' His body shook as he rolled her on to her side and his hand stroked her thigh, lifting it. 'Like it? Yes, I liked it,' he told her roughly as he started to move against her.

'But you didn't show it. You didn't hold me against you the way you did when I sucked you here,' she told him, touching his nipple.

Her voice had become breathy and soft as she felt him enter her.

'That wasn't because I didn't want to. It was because I dared not,' Guard told her rawly. 'Did you want me to?'

'Yes,' Rosy admitted. 'Yes, Guard, it made me want you so much.'

'That's good,' Guard told her, 'because it certainly made me want you.'

As he moved inside her, Rosy wrapped herself blissfully around him.

'Oh, Guard, that feels so good...so good...so good.'

'Still love me...?'

Sleepily, Rosy opened her eyes. She was lying curled up against Guard's body where she had fallen asleep after the last time they had made love.

'Mmm... More than ever,' she told him. 'Do you love me?'

'Yes,' Guard told her quietly. 'Above and beyond anything else there ever has been in my life or ever will be. You *are* my life, Rosy. My life and my love. Today, tomorrow, always and for ever. I love you.'

BRIDE'S BAY RESORT

UNLOCK THE DOOR TO GREAT ROMANCE AT BRIDE'S BAY RESORT

Join Harlequin's new across-the-lines series, set in an exclusive hotel on an island off the coast of South Carolina.

Seven of your favorite authors will bring you exciting stories about fascinating heroes and heroines discovering love at Bride's Bay Resort.

Look for these fabulous stories coming to a store near you beginning in January 1996.

Harlequin American Romance #613 in January
Matchmaking Baby by Cathy Gillen Thacker

Harlequin Presents #1794 in February
Indiscretions by Robyn Donald

Harlequin Intrigue #362 in March
Love and Lies by Dawn Stewardson

Harlequin Romance #3404 in April
Make Believe Engagement by Day Leclaire

Harlequin Temptation #588 in May
Stranger in the Night by Roseanne Williams

Harlequin Superromance #695 in June
Married to a Stranger by Connie Bennett

Harlequin Historicals #324 in July
Dulcie's Gift by Ruth Langan

Visit Bride's Bay Resort each month wherever Harlequin books are sold.

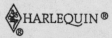

HARLEQUIN®

BBAYG

HARLEQUIN ⬦ PRESENTS®

brings you

Second Honeymoon
by
Sandra Field

The second book in her great new series,
Significant Others. A series that celebrates the magical
mayhem of modern relationships and follows the loves,
lives and passionate adventures of Lucy Barnes and
her sister Marcia.

In *Beyond Reach*, Lucy was a happy bride—now she's
a runaway wife! Could her estranged husband,
Troy Donovan, be just the guy to catch her? Lucy has
turned her back on love—it hurts too much. It's hardly
an invitation for a second honeymoon, but Troy needs his
wife back or out of his system for good. He's determined
to get what he wants—even if it means seducing his
own wife....

The exciting sequel to *Beyond Reach!*

"Sandra Field pens a phenomenal love story...
pure pleasure."   —*Romantic Times*

Sandra Field's page-turning new trilogy:

*First they were strangers, then they were lovers, now
they're Significant Others!*